e. l. konigsburg

SCHOLASTIC INC.

New York Toronto London Auckland Sydney
Mexico City New Delhi Hong Kong Buenos Aires

ISBN 0-439-31698-7

12 11 10 9 8 7 6 5 4 3 2 1   1 2 3 4 5 6/0

Printed in the U.S.A.   37

First Scholastic printing, September 2001

Book design by Ann Bobco
The text of this book is set in Perpetua.

For:
Anna F. Konigsburg,
Sarah L. Konigsburg,
and
Meg L. Konigsburg
—until eponymy

SILENT TO THE BONE

DAYS ONE, TWO, & THREE

1

It is easy to pinpoint the minute when my friend Branwell began his silence. It was Wednesday, November 25, 2:43 P.M., Eastern Standard Time. It was there—or, I guess you could say not there—on the tape of the 911 call.

Operator: *Epiphany 911. Hobson speaking.*
SILENCE.
Operator: *Epiphany 911. Hobson. May I help you?*
SILENCE. [Voices are heard in the background.]
Operator: *Anyone there?*
A woman's voice [screaming in the background]: *Tell them. Tell them.*
Operator: *Ma'am, I can't hear you.* [then louder] *Please come to the phone.*

<u>A woman's voice</u> [still in the background, but louder now]: *Tell them.* [then, screaming as the voice approaches] *For God's sake, Branwell.* [the voice gets louder] *TELL THEM.*

SILENCE.

<u>Operator</u>: *Please speak into the phone.*

<u>A woman's voice</u> [heard more clearly]: *TELL THEM. NOW, BRAN. TELL THEM NOW.*

SILENCE.

<u>A woman's voice with a British accent</u> [heard clearly]: *Here! Take her! For God's sake, at least take her!* [then, speaking directly into the phone] *It's the baby. She won't wake up.*

<u>Operator</u>: *Stay on the phone.*

<u>British Accent</u> [frightened]: *The baby won't wake up.*

<u>Operator</u>: *Stay on the line. We're transferring you to Fire and Rescue.*

<u>Male Voice</u>: *Epiphany Fire and Rescue. Davidson. What is the nature of your emergency?*

<u>British Accent</u>: *The baby won't wake up.*

<u>Male Voice</u>: *What is your exact location?*

<u>British Accent</u>: *198 Tower Hill Road. Help, please. It's the baby.*

<u>Male Voice</u>: *Help is on the way, ma'am. What happened?*

<u>British Accent</u>: *He dropped her. She won't wake up.*

<u>Male Voice</u>: *Is she having difficulty breathing?*

<u>British Accent</u> [panicky now]: *Yes. Her breathing is all strange.*

<u>Male Voice</u>: *How old is the baby, ma'am?*

<u>British Accent</u>: *Almost six months.*

<u>Male Voice</u>: *Is there a history of asthma or heart trouble?*

<u>British Accent</u>: *No, no. He dropped her, I tell you.*

LOUD BANGING IS HEARD.

<u>British Accent</u> [into the phone]: *They're here. Thank God. They're here.* [then just before the connection is broken] *For God's sake, Branwell, MOVE. Open the door.*

The SILENCES were Branwell's. He is my friend.

The baby was Nicole—called Nikki—Branwell's half sister.

The British accent was Vivian Shawcurt, the babysitter.

In the ambulance en route to the hospital, Vivian sat up front with the driver, who was also a paramedic. He asked her what had happened. She told him that she had put the baby down for her afternoon nap and had gone to her room. After talking to a friend on the phone, she had started to read and must have dozed off. When the paramedic asked her what time that was, she had to confess that she did not know. The next thing she remembered being awakened by

Branwell's screaming for her. Something was wrong with the baby. When she came into the nursery, she saw Branwell shaking Nikki, trying to get her to wake up. She guessed that the baby went unconscious when he dropped her. She started to do CPR and told Branwell to call 911. He did, but when the operator came on the line, he seemed paralyzed. He would not give her the information she needed. He would not speak at all.

Meanwhile the paramedic who rode with the baby in the ambulance was following the ABC's for resuscitation—airway, breathing, and circulation. Once inside the trauma center at Clarion County Hospital, Nikki was put on a respirator and wrapped in blankets. It was important to keep her warm. A CAT scan was taken of her head, which showed that her injuries could cause her brain to swell. When the brain swells, it pushes against the skull, and that squeezes the blood vessels that supply the brain. If the supply of blood to the brain is pinched off, the brain cannot get oxygen, and it dies.

The doctor drilled a hole in Nikki's skull and put in a small tube—no thicker than a strand of spaghetti—to drain excess fluid from her brain to lower the pressure. Nikki did not open her eyes.

Later that afternoon, a police car arrived at 198 Tower Hill Road and took Branwell to the Clarion County Juvenile Behavioral Center. He said nothing. Nothing to the doctors. Nothing to his father, to his stepmother. Calling to Vivian was the last that Branwell had spoken. He had not uttered a sound since dialing 911.

Dr. Zamborska, Branwell's father, asked me to visit him at the Behavioral Center and see if I could get him to talk. I am Connor, Connor Kane, and—except for the past six weeks or so—Branwell and I had always been best friends.

When Dr. Z called me, he reported that the pressure in Nikki's skull was dropping, and that was a good sign, but, he cautioned, she was still in a coma. She was in critical condition, and there was no way of knowing what the outcome would be.

I was not allowed to see Branwell until Friday, the day after Thanksgiving. On that first visit to the Behavioral Center and on all the visits that followed, I had to stop at a reception desk and sign in. There I would empty my pockets and, when I had my backpack with me, I would have to open it as well. If I had nothing that could cause harm to Branwell or could let him cause harm to someone else (I never did), I was allowed to put it all back and take it with me.

That first time the guard brought Branwell into the visitors' room, he looked awful. His hair was greasy and uncombed, and he was so pale that the orange jumpsuit he wore cast an apricot glow up from his chin just as his red hair seemed to cast the same eerie glow across his forehead. He shuffled as he walked toward me. I saw that his shoes had no laces. I guessed they had taken them from him.

Branwell is tall for his age—I am not—and when he sat across the table from me, I had to look up to make eye contact, which was not easy. His eyeglasses were so badly smudged that his blue eyes appeared almost gray. It was not at all like him to be uncombed and to have his glasses smeared like that. I guessed the smudges were to keep him from seeing out, just as his silence was to keep him from speaking out.

On that first awful, awkward visit, a uniformed guard stood leaning against the wall, watching us. There was no one else in the visitors' room, and I was the only one talking, so everything I said, every sound I made, seemed to echo off the walls. I felt so responsible for getting Branwell to talk that I asked him a bunch of dumb questions. Like: What happened? And:

Was there anything he wanted to tell me? He, of course, didn't utter a sound. Zombielike, he slowly, slowly, slowly shook his head once, twice, three times. This was not the Branwell I knew, and yet, strangely, it was.

Dr. Zamborska had asked me to visit Bran because he figured that I probably knew Branwell better than anyone else in Epiphany—except for himself. And because we had always seemed to have a lot to say to each other. We both loved to talk, but Branwell loved it more. He loved words. He had about five words for things that most people had only one word for, and could use four of five in a single sentence. Dr. Z probably figured that if anyone could get Bran to talk, it would be me. Talk was like the vitamins of our friendship: Large daily doses kept it healthy.

But when Dr. Z had asked me to visit Branwell, he didn't know that about six weeks before that 911 call something had changed between us. I didn't know what caused it, and I didn't exactly know how to describe it. We had not had a fight or even a quarrel, but ever since Monday, Columbus Day, October 12, something that had always been between us no longer was. We still walked to the school bus stop together, we still got off at the same stop, and we still talked.

But Branwell never seemed to start a conversation anymore. He not only had less time for me, he also had less to say to me, which, in terms of our friendship, was pretty much the same thing. He seemed to have something hidden.

We had both turned thirteen within three weeks of each other, and at first I wondered if he was entering a new phase of development three weeks ahead of me. Was something happening to him that would happen to me three weeks later? Had he started to shave? I looked real close. He hadn't. (I was relieved.) Had he become a moody teenager, and would I become one in three more weeks? Three weeks passed, and I didn't. Then six weeks passed—the six weeks between Columbus Day and that 911 call—and I still had not caught the moodiness that was deepening in my friend. And I still did not know what was happening to Bran.

After that first strange, clouded visit, I decided that if I was going back (and I knew that I would), nothing good was going to come out of my visits unless I forgot about our estrangement, forgot about having an assignment from Dr. Z, and acted like the old friend I was.

*　　*　　*

Once on our way to the school bus stop in the days when Branwell was still starting conversations, he asked me a famous question: "If a tree falls in the forest and no one is there to hear it, does it make a sound?" When he asked me, I couldn't answer and neither could he, but when I left him that first Friday of his long silence, I thought that Branwell could answer it. On that day and for all the days that followed when he made no sound, my friend Branwell was screaming on the inside. And no one heard.

Except me.

So when Branwell at last broke his silence, I was there. I was the first to hear him speak. He spoke to me because even before I knew the details, I believed in him. I knew that Branwell did not hurt that baby.

I won't say what his first words were until I explain what I heard during the time he said nothing.

DAYS
      BEFORE
DAY   ONE.

2.

I cannot explain why Branwell and I became friends. I don't think there is a *why* for friendship, and if I try to come up with reasons why we should be friends, I can come up with as many reasons why we should not be. But I can be definite about the where and the when. *Where:* nursery school. *When:* forever.

I've mentioned that we are practically the same age—he's three weeks older—and since the day I was born, our paths have crossed. Often. We both have fathers who work at the university. We both live on Tower Hill Road on the edge of the campus, and we both spent our nursery school and kindergarten days at the university lab school. Friendship depends on interlocking time, place, and state of mind.

These are some of the differences between us. Branwell was raised by a single parent, but I have always had a mother. Branwell is the product of a first wife; I am the product of a second. Branwell's half sister is younger; mine is older. There was divorce in my family. There was a death in his.

Branwell's mother was killed in an auto accident when he was nine months old. His father was driving. Three blocks from their house, he was blindsided by a drunk driver. His mother was in the passenger seat up front. Branwell was in the back, buckled into the best, most expensive, safest car seat in the world, which had been a gift from the Branwells, his mother's parents.

There were times when Branwell thought that he remembered nothing about the accident, but he had been told about it so often that there were other times when he was not sure if he remembered being there or being told he was. My mother, who has a master's degree in psychology, says that Dr. Zamborska has never stopped wishing that he had been killed instead of his wife. Branwell would appreciate knowing that there is a name for those feelings: *survivor guilt*. My mother told me that whole books have been written about it.

The differences in our families are not enough to

explain why we should not be friends any more than the similarities between us are enough to explain why we should be. Let me put it this way: The big difference between Branwell Zamborska and me is Branwell himself. Branwell is just plain different. First of all, he stands out in any crowd. For one thing he is tall, and for another he has bright red hair. But even those things don't explain his differences.

Branwell drops his books—usually all of them—at least five times a day. If he's talking to you, and he's in the middle of a sentence, and he drops his books, he picks them up and finishes his sentence without stopping.

Branwell cannot hit a ball with a bat or get one into a basket, and he is never on the A-list when kids are picking players for a makeup game of soccer or softball. When he isn't picked, he seems just as happy to watch as to play.

Branwell has very long legs, and he can run. Actually, he's a very good runner. But when he runs, he looks like a camel—all knobby-kneed and loose-jointed with his neck stretched so far out that his nose is over the goal line five minutes before his shoulders. So most people comment on his gait rather than his speed—even though he often wins, places, or shows.

Branwell is very good at music. He plays the piano and has an excellent singing voice. But even his taste in music is offbeat. He loves Mozart and Beethoven and the Beatles—all the classics—and doesn't know that Red Hot Chili Peppers and Pearl Jam are musical groups and not ingredients and that Smashing Pumpkins is not directions for using them. And—most offbeat of all—he doesn't care that he doesn't know.

Earlier this year we were studying the American Civil War. The teacher asked, "What was the Missouri Compromise?" Branwell had his hand up, so the teacher called on him. Instead of answering the question, he asked one: "Have you read *A Stillness at Appomattox*?" She hadn't read it, and Branwell said, as innocently as you please, "An excellent book. I highly recommend it."

Branwell (1) Did not realize that he had not answered the teacher's question. (2) Did not realize that he was making the teacher uncomfortable because he had read a grown-up book that she probably should have read and hadn't. (3) Did not say the book was *neat* or *cool;* he said it was excellent and that he highly recommended it. (4) Did not realize that he was treating the teacher like his equal. (5) Did not realize that the teacher didn't think he was her equal and did not like being treated as if she were.

No one in the class ever mentioned (1) through (5) because we were proud to have someone in our class smart enough to recommend *A Stillness at Appomattox* to our social studies teacher.

Last year we were asked to write essays about freedom for a contest sponsored by our local Rotary Club for the Martin Luther King, Jr. holiday. I wrote about the Freedom Riders who rode buses through the South in 1961 challenging segregated seating, rest rooms, and drinking fountains. There was a lot of stuff in the library about them. Branwell wrote about the Four Freedoms of World War II: freedom of speech and expression, freedom of worship, freedom from want, and freedom from fear. He wrote about each of those freedoms and how they were the basic reasons wars were fought. You could say that his essay was philosophical; mine was historical. His was long; mine was short. Mine was good; his was better. Mine won. When I won, my mother was proud and happy. My father was proud and happy. But no one was prouder of me or happier for me than Branwell, and I think he would not have been prouder or happier if he had won himself. And I don't know anyone anywhere who has a friend like that.

Until Dr. Zamborska met and married Tina Nguyen and except for the month of July when Branwell was sent to Florida to spend time with his mother's parents, father and son went everywhere together. When Branwell was a baby and if Dr. Z's research required that he return to the lab in the evening, he took Branwell with him—even if it was midnight. If he was scheduled to give a paper at a conference of geneticists, he took Branwell along even if it meant that Branwell had to miss a day of school. Dr. Zamborska never missed a single teacher-parent conference, Disney movie, school play, or soccer game.

My mother told me that even when Branwell was an infant, Dr. Z would bicycle over from his lab to feed him. He sat in the nursing room among the women who were nursing their babies—she herself was one—to give Branwell his bottle. Dr. Zamborska is tall like Branwell, and has red hair like him. He stands out in any crowd, but in that room of nursing mothers, he hardly seemed out of place because after only a few visits, the nursing mothers stopped being embarrassed and considered him one of them and exchanged information about Pampers and pacifiers.

When Branwell rides his bike, he gets his pants leg caught in the chain of his bicycle. When he sits next to you in the bleachers, he sits too close. When he laughs at one of your jokes, he laughs too loud. When he eats a peanut butter and jelly sandwich, he ends up with a pound of peanut butter caught in his braces.

When he sits too close, I tell him to back off. When he has peanut butter stuck in his braces, I tell him to clean it up. When he gets his pants leg caught in his bicycle chain, I stop and wait for him to get untangled.

I figure that Branwell got his awkwardness from his father, and I guess I got my acceptance from my mother. And here's the final thing I have to say about being friends with Branwell. He is different, but no one messes with him because everyone knows there is a lot to Branwell besides the sitting-too-close and the laughing-too-loud. They just don't choose to be his friend. But I do. Who else would invite a guy over to hear his new CD of Mozart's Prague Symphony and let him listen without having to pretend that he likes it or pretend that he doesn't? Who else would ask a question like "If a tree falls in the forest and no one is there to hear it, does it make a sound?" the first thing in the morning?

Branwell had always been fascinated with words and names. He liked to name things. When his dad and Tina found out that the baby would be a girl, they drew up a long list of possible names and studied it for a long time. They decided on Nicole, Nikki for short. Branwell liked the name. Liked it a lot, but when they asked him what he thought of it, he didn't say much except, "Nice." They thought Branwell was only luke-warm about it, but the exact opposite was true. Bran-well liked the name *Nicole—Nikki*—very much, but his answer had little to do with the question. He was try-ing to tell them how disappointed he was that he had not been part of the decision. Dr. Z must have forgot-ten how much Branwell loved naming things, and Tina never got to know him well enough to find out.

Branwell likes his own name because it was his mother's before she got married. She was Linda Bran-well, an only child. She was tall, and she also wore glasses at an early age. He calls his mother's parents The Ancestors. They think that except for the red hair, which he got from his father and which they don't mention, Branwell looks like her, and judging from the photos that I've seen, I would agree.

Branwell spent every July with them at The Lovely Condominium, which is the name he has given to the place where they live. His grandfather Branwell re-tired to Naples, Florida after being an executive with General Motors. In addition to a beach, The Lovely

Condominium complex has everything their Beautiful Home in Bloomfield Hills had. It has its own golf course, club house, tennis courts, and swimming pool. Dr. Zamborska says that the chemicals it takes to keep the pool, golf course, and grounds lovely would fertilize the wheat fields of a small nation. But Dr. Z does not say such things to The Ancestors, just as they don't say anything about Branwell's red hair. He is a gentle man, and he knows how much they love Branwell, and how much they miss Linda because he does, too. So he sends Branwell to them every July where Branwell is expected to do very grown-up things like playing golf and dressing for dinner. Branwell is no better at golf or tennis than he is at basketball, but for the entire month he spends with them, he never gives up trying to be what they want him to be.

Every November—save the one with the infamous 911 call—Dr. Zamborska and Branwell traveled to Pittsburgh to spend Thanksgiving with his father's parents. Dr. Zamborska is one of four children—all living—and Branwell is one of seven grandchildren on that side of the family. I have never met Branwell's cousins, but I'll bet he stands out in that crowd as much as he does in any other—even though I've heard they are all tall and have red hair.

It's strange that someone like Branwell who loves words so much would be silent. In the early days of Branwell's silence, I wondered—in light of Nikki's injury—if a new generation of survivor guilt had spilled over into him. Was he trying to make himself unconscious like Nikki? In the weeks that followed, I discovered that the reasons for his not speaking were layered. He could not speak until the last layer had been peeled away and laid aside.

I am proud to say that the first words he spoke were to me, which does not help explain why we are friends but it says a lot about how deep the layers of our friendship go.

DAY FOUR

3.

The next time I went to see Branwell, Dr. Zamborska was just leaving. He had rushed over to the Behavioral Center to tell Branwell the good news. The doctor had pinched Nikki below her collarbone, and her hand had reached toward the pinch. That showed a new level of consciousness. Even better, she was fluttering her eyes. Everyone hoped that this was a preview to her actually opening her eyes.

Dr. Z told me that Branwell had been following instructions, going through the motions. Showered when told to. Ate—not much but enough—when food was put in front of him. He thought that Branwell was looking a little better, but the good news about Nikki didn't do a thing to break his silence. He still had not uttered a sound.

Dr. Z had hired a lawyer, Gretchen Silver, to defend Bran if the state brought charges against him. All that would depend on what happened to Nikki. I wondered how any lawyer—or anyone—could possibly defend Bran if he wouldn't say anything?

When the guard brought Branwell into the visitors' room, he still looked pale, but his glasses were not smudged now, and I could see his eyes. I told him how glad I was that Nikki had fluttered her eyes. And that's when the idea came to me.

Branwell could speak to me with his eyes.

There was a way we could communicate.

My mother belongs to a book club and always reads the reviews in the Sunday *New York Times* so that she can make suggestions to her group. One Sunday, she told Dad and me about a book that had just been "written" by a Frenchman who was totally paralyzed, except for his left eye, which he was able to blink. I remember the name of the book because it was unusual. It was called *The Diving Bell and the Butterfly*. This man—his last name was Bauby—wrote the whole book by having a friend recite the alphabet to him, and when she came to the letter he wanted, he would blink that left eye.

The following Monday on the way to the bus stop, I

26

had mentioned this to Branwell and asked him if he thought you could say the man actually *wrote* the book. Maybe this wasn't as philosophical a question as "When a tree falls in a forest . . . ," but it did make him think about what it meant to "write" a book. Bran decided that if someone dictates a letter that someone else writes or types, the *writer* is the one who puts the words together. Because of what he had said about a writer being the one who puts words together, I knew that he couldn't write any more than he could speak.

But the words were in him. I knew they were. All those words he loved and all those names he made up were in him, but it was as if they had gotten crushed in a Cuisinart. Their sounds—all their sounds—had blended together and become a mush that he could not sort into syllables. They had become sounds he could neither separate nor say.

He was still robot-like, but his eyes had become more alive. I thought, What if I made a series of flash cards and spread them out on the table and watched which ones make Branwell's eyes flutter?

Anything I wrote to him or he wrote to me would be watched by the guard, but, I thought, who could he report to? And what would the person really know if he did? And, besides, guards are not snitches. Isn't there some law that protects the privacy of people in public places?

That evening, I cut up the cardboard backing of two yellow tablets. I measured them into thirds the long way and into halves the short way. That gave me six cards per tablet-back. Twelve cards in all. Two sides to a card. I had room for twenty-four things, but I decided to start with one side. Twelve things.

I wrote names and phrases that I thought would jog him into speaking again. I wrote things as they came to me. Like those association tests given by my mother who is getting her doctorate in psychology. She shows or tells someone a word like *butter* or *beach,* and they are supposed to write or say all the words that come to mind when they see that word.

I wrote BLUE PETER first. A *blue peter* is a blue flag with a white square in the center, and it is flown when a ship is ready to sail. That had become a code word between Branwell and me last summer when he had come back from a cruise of the Caribbean. Branwell lives at 198 Tower Hill Road, and I live at 184. His house is farther from the school bus stop than mine, so in the mornings when he left his house, he had taken to calling me and saying, "Blue peter"—nothing more—and hanging up. That's how I would know that he was ready to leave for the bus stop. That gave me time to gather my books, put on my jacket, and walk to the end of our driveway where I would meet him.

Blue Peter made me think of school. So the next card I wrote was DAY CARE, which is what Bran and I called school.

On another, I wrote SIAS. That was what we called a game we played on the way to the bus stop. It means Summarize In A Sentence. For example, I would say to Branwell, "The movie *Titanic*. SIAS." That movie was a big hit that summer. Bran came up with this: "Rich girl escapes while poor artist drowns when mega-ship sees only the tip of the iceberg and sinks as the crew rearranges the deck chairs while the band plays on." Bran got four stars, our highest rating, for that SIAS because although we deduct for *ands*—he had used one—we also award extra points for clichés, and he had managed to work three into one SIAS.

I stacked the cards and fastened them together with a rubber band and put them in my backpack. They were Connor Kane's secret entry cards in the Break-the-Silence Sweepstakes Challenge. They would become my means of communicating with Branwell.

DAY FIVE

4.

Nikki opened her eyes. She moved her feet and arms. Her brain was reestablishing cycles of sleeping and waking, which meant a new level of consciousness. The doctors were no longer concerned about the pressure inside her skull. (That tiny tube they had put inside her brain could also monitor the pressure.) Everyone celebrated, but the doctors warned that although she was technically no longer in a coma, she could not follow commands and still had a long, long way to go.

The first thing I did on my next visit to the Behavioral Center was mention the good news about Nikki's opening her eyes. But I'm sure that Branwell already knew, because I thought there was more spring and less shuffle in his step when the guard brought him out.

I spread the flash cards out on the table between us. As I laid them out, I explained, "Remember the story of the paralyzed Frenchman who wrote a whole book with the blink of his left eye?" I no sooner had the sentence out of my mouth than Branwell blinked his eyes twice, very rapidly, and I knew he understood the rules of our communication.

First, I let him look them all over. Even though he hardly shifted his head as he looked at them, I felt confident that I would get a signal. I didn't know which card it would be, but I was sure it would be one. He lowered his head slightly, and I read that as a signal that he was ready. I pointed to the cards, one at a time.

He blinked twice at one of the cards. His choice surprised me. I gathered them together, putting that one on top. It was MARGARET. I held the deck out with that one card facing him. He blinked twice again. I said, "Okay, we'll start with Margaret."

I dropped the cards into my backpack and was out the door of the Behavioral Center when I realized that I didn't quite know what to do with MARGARET. Just looking at the card sure didn't make him speak. Was she possibly the person he wanted to speak to? Or was she the one who would tell me why he could not? Why MARGARET?

Margaret is my half sister. She is fourteen years older than me. She runs her own computer consulting business out of an old house on Schuyler Place that she inherited from her two great-uncles. Schuyler Place is in Old Town, the oldest residential section of Epiphany across the campus from Tower Hill Road. The main buildings of Old Town line up around a small square park. This is where the townspeople shopped before they started building malls. The old city hall faces the square, and so does the original Carnegie Library.

Margaret's house, like all the others in Old Town, has a front porch, and the street itself has sidewalks on both sides of the road. In a strip of dirt between the sidewalk and the curb there are trees that were planted a hundred years ago when the university was just a college and people walked to classes and to the grocery store. In the summer when the trees are in full leaf, they make a canopy over the road—which, these days, is only wide enough for one-way traffic.

Like a lot of doctors and lawyers who have bought these old houses, Margaret converted the living room and dining room into offices, rewired the whole house, remodeled the kitchen, and added on a room and a terrace in the back. There are three bedrooms—two small, one medium—and a bathroom upstairs. You can do whatever you want to the inside of the house, but you are not allowed to change the front that faces the street, and you even have to have the city approve of the colors you want to paint it. Some of the doctors and lawyers who opened offices in Old Town don't live there, but Margaret does.

The backs of the houses in Old Town face an alley, and that is where the people park their cars and put out their garbage on garbage-collection days. Despite not having enough parking space, Margaret loves the house, the location, the alley behind it, and every brick in the sidewalk in front. She says that Tower Hill Road is a nice place to visit, but she doesn't want to live there.

Margaret and I had always liked each other but it wasn't until the first Thursday of Knightsbridge Middle School that we became good friends. Old Town and Knightsbridge, where I attend eighth grade, are both on the side of campus that is opposite our house. They are walking distance from each other and from the Behavioral Center.

It was raining that first Thursday, and I had missed

the school bus home. That was the first year my mother had gone back to the university to get her doctorate. She had a class on Thursday afternoons and was not scheduled to be home until four, the time the bus would normally drop me off. Unprepared for a two-and-a-half-mile trek across campus in the rain, I decided to walk the short distance to Schuyler Place, where I could call my mother and wait out of the rain.

Margaret welcomed me as if I were a walk-in customer even though in her business there aren't any walk-ins since everything is done by appointment. She told me to call my mother and tell her that she would drive me home as soon as she finished work. In the meantime, I should go on back and make myself at home. Which I did.

I got into the habit of stopping at Schuyler Place every Thursday after school. In little ways Margaret let me know that she liked my company. She lay in a supply of after-school snacks, and she gave me a key to the back door, the one that opened the add-on living room. Even on the Thursdays when she was busy in the office, she would take time to come on back to say hi and to ask me how school was. And we both began to take it for granted that she would drive me home.

After seeing Branwell at the Behavioral Center the

day that he had chosen MARGARET, I decided to stop at her place and talk to her about him and tell her what I was trying to do.

Margaret was tied up in the office, so I went to hang out in the add-on living room, as I usually did. I was glad to be left alone. If you're a guy and not a girl, and you're my age—just weeks past thirteen—you're too old to have a baby-sitter but too young to be one. So to be left really alone is like a gift of civil rights.

I have mentioned that one of the things that Branwell and I have always had in common is that both of our fathers work at the university. My dad, Roderick Kane, is the registrar. He keeps the university records. He doesn't teach. He is an administrator.

Branwell's dad, Dr. Stefan Zamborska, is a well-known geneticist. He is a doctor of philosophy, a Ph.D. He teaches one class a semester, but most of his time is spent in the Biotech Lab, working on the Genome Project. If you ask him what he does, Dr. Z will tell you that he is a map maker. And that is true. He is part of the team that is making a map of all the genes in the human body. Dr. Z is well-respected in his field. Which means that he is somewhat famous. *Somewhat famous* means that *People* magazine is not likely to write a story about him, but *The Journal of Genetic Research* will print anything he has to say.

Dr. Zamborska is admired by the people he works with, not only for the work he does but also for the kind of parent he is. He arranged for baby-sitters only when absolutely necessary, and most often the baby-sitter he asked was my half sister, Margaret.

Margaret's mother is another Ph.D.—there are always a lot of them around a university. She is a professor in the psychology department, where she supervises students who are getting master's degrees. When Margaret was twelve years old, my mother was one of her mother's graduate students. It doesn't take advanced math to figure out how my father met my mother and how Margaret wound up being my half sister.

Margaret was visiting Tower Hill Road the night that Mrs. Zamborska was killed. The accident happened on the Saturday night of a weekend when Dad had visiting privileges. My mother and father took Branwell in while Dr. Zamborska went to the hospital with his wife. Margaret always said that that was when she bonded with Branwell and began her career as his chief (and usually *only*) baby-sitter.

Margaret never baby-sat for my father, but she often

did for Branwell's. Her visits to our house were just that—*visits.* I like Margaret, and she likes me, but she doesn't like my mother. I like my mother very much and can understand why my father prefers mine to hers, but I can also understand why Margaret doesn't. I guess she figured that baby-sitting for me would be doing a favor for my mother, and when she came to our house on Tower Hill Road she wanted to be her father's daughter, not my mother's helper.

When Margaret came back to the add-on living room, she poured us each a glass of cold cider, and we sat at the kitchen table and talked. I told her about making out the cards and how I had put her name on one and how Branwell had chosen her. I asked her if she could tell me why.

"Because I was there."

"Where?"

"Let's first talk about when."

The summer before last when Branwell returned home from The Lovely Condominium, Dr. Zamborska asked Margaret to meet Branwell at the airport. She didn't mind that Dr. Zamborska still thought of her as his baby-sitter and actually was pleased that he felt that he could still call on her when he needed help.

When Branwell got off the plane, he was surprised to see Margaret instead of his father, but Margaret told him that his dad was stuck in a meeting. She had not seen Bran for several months and thought he was looking good and told him so. The Ancestors had sent him home dressed in a navy blue blazer, a white shirt with a button-down collar, and a necktie. Most kids would have taken off the necktie as soon as the plane took off, but not Branwell. He was the good grandson all the way home. With his fair skin and red hair, Branwell never tanned, but after a month in the Florida sun—even with double-digit sunblock—he had freckled. When he reached over the carousel to retrieve his bag, Margaret noticed a band of sunburn across the back of his neck. She said, "You'll have to get a havelock."

Branwell replied, "Yeah, either that or let my hair grow long."

Margaret said that she thought Branwell was probably the only kid in this state who would know what she meant. Being a little disappointed that she didn't think I would also know—I didn't—I asked her what a havelock was. She told me that it was a cap that has a flap of cloth attached to cover the neck, named after Sir Henry Havelock, the man who invented it. "Like a sandwich is named after the Earl of Sandwich."(I didn't know that either.)

It was the last Friday in July, the sidewalks were still soaking up summer heat, and the house on Tower Hill Road felt stuffy—unused—when they got there. Branwell looked around expectantly. Margaret knew he was looking for his father, whom he thought would be looking for him expectantly. Of course, in the past Dr. Z had always met his plane, waiting at the gate, craning his neck to look down the jetway to get a first glimpse of him. When Bran didn't find his father downstairs, he went upstairs to get rid of his suitcase and to use the bathroom. While he was upstairs, Dr. Zamborska returned home, and Branwell came flying down the stairs to see him but stopped short, halfway down, for his father was not alone. Standing beside him was Dr. Tina Nguyen. Tina.

Margaret told me, "The look on Branwell's face brought tears to my eyes." I asked her why, and she studied me a long time before she answered, "Because I had been there. I recognized the look."

Then—right then and there—just thinking about it made Margaret's eyes fill with tears again—right there in front of me. She sniffed the tears back and said, "I remembered coming home from summer camp when I was twelve years old. I remembered coming downstairs for supper that evening. I remembered going into the family room, where my parents usually had a glass of wine before dinner. And I remembered seeing them there: Mom and Dad and your mother. I had not seen my parents for a month, and I had hoped to have them to myself that evening. But I looked over at my dad—our dad—and I think I knew, even before my mother did, that we were never again going to be the same kind of family we had been."

"Is that when Dad moved out?"

"Not quite. He waited until the fall term was over. He moved out at the first of the year, right after Christmas break. But from that evening on, I knew it was only a matter of time before he would. So when I saw Branwell come down the stairs to find his father with Tina, I knew that he knew. I knew what he was feeling. Branwell knew, just as I had known, that it would be only a matter of time before Tina would move in, and they would be a different kind of family from what they had been before. I had once been in that same sad place.

"Then Dr. Zamborska said, 'We thought we'd go out

for dinner this evening, Bran.' Branwell smiled and said something to the effect that The Ancestors did a lot of eating out. 'Mostly at the clubhouse.' Then he smiled and said, 'I'll just go upstairs to take off my jacket, and then I'll be blue peter.'"

I asked Margaret if that was the first that she had heard of blue peter, and she said it was. I asked her if she knew what it meant, and she told me that she guessed.

"Couldn't you find it on the Internet?" I asked. (Margaret spends almost all her waking hours on the Internet.)

"Didn't try."

"Want me to tell you?"

"I know you're dying to."

"It means 'ready to sail.' When a ship is ready to sail, it flies a blue flag with a white square that stands for the letter P—blue peter. Is that what you guessed?"

"I guessed it meant 'ready.' You didn't ask me if I guessed whether it had to do with sailing ships."

"I thought you'd like to know."

"It's not that my life would have been unfulfilled and empty if I had never known, but if you had not had this wonderful opportunity to tell me, yours might have been. Now, do you want me to tell you about the rest of that evening when I picked Branwell up from the airport?"

"Blue peter," I said.

"I hope that means you're ready to listen."

"It doesn't mean that I'm ready to sail."

"I guessed as much," Margaret said. "Dr. Zamborska started to say something, and I knew what it would be. He was about to tell Branwell that he hadn't planned on Branwell's joining them, that he had planned on just him and Tina going out. But before he could even start to say it, I got to his side and poked him with my elbow to interrupt. 'Now that everyone is together,' I said, 'I guess I'll be running along.' And I was out the door before either Dr. Z or Tina had a chance to reply.

"He had asked me to stay to baby-sit. He had been planning to take Tina out to the Summit Inn, where you do have to wear a jacket and tie. I found out later that he had a ring in his pocket and had planned on asking Tina to marry him that very night. But when I saw that look on Branwell's face, a look I recognized from my own personal wardrobe of bad memories, I decided that it would be wrong for them to leave him—especially on his first night home. So I walked out. I left Dr. Z to work out the details. He quietly canceled his reservations at the Summit, and they all went to One-Potato for supper."

Even before he had left for his month with The Ancestors, Branwell knew who Tina Nguyen was. She was part of his father's research team.

Dr. Zamborska's research is funded by the National Institutes of Health in Washington, D.C. They pay for three assistants. The assistants are graduate students who help Dr. Zamborska's research while they study for advanced degrees. They spend an average of four years studying with him. Each time one graduates, others apply for the job. Dr. Z is known as a fair but strict teacher and mentor. Many apply, but only one is chosen.

Dr. Zamborska never dated any of them. He never went out with anyone he had worked with, but Tina was something different. For one thing, she was not a student.

Tina Nguyen represented something new in Dr. Z's lab as well as in his life. She was already a Ph.D. when she arrived at the university. She was a molecular biologist working on identifying genes associated with complex genetic traits. She answered an ad that Dr. Zamborska had put in *The Journal of Genetic Research* because she wanted a challenge. She came to work at the start of the summer term in June, and they had gone out together a couple of times even before Bran had to leave for Florida. Bran never told me much about Tina except to say that she had a lot in common with his father. She was brilliant. She was interested in the Genome. And she rode a bicycle everywhere.

What Bran didn't know was how much time they had been spending together in the lab, cultivating more than just DNA.

I was at summer camp part of the time that Bran-well was at The Lovely Condominium. I left home a week before he did, so I got home a week before him, and when I did, you had only to see Tina and Dr. Zam-borska together to know how full of each other they were. They could hardly keep their hands off each other, which made a lot of people smile, but to tell you the truth, I found it a little embarrassing, and I wondered if Branwell would, too.

Margaret said, "I have no doubt that Dr. Zamborska is brilliant, but he is also stupid. He had always treated Branwell like a grown-up, and I guess he thought that Branwell would take the news like a man, but he had no business letting all that love between him and Tina ripen while Branwell was away and never even sending out a hint. When our father abandoned me, I at least still had a mother. But when Dr. Zamborska fell in love with Tina, Branwell was just left out."

DAY EIGHT

5.

There was good news about Nikki. The pressure inside her skull had gone down and stayed down, and the doctor removed the tube from her brain. When the guard brought Branwell into the visitors' room, I got the feeling that he was glad to see me. It could only be a feeling, because he certainly wasn't telling me so, but something positive was definitely there, and I don't think there is any feeling I like more than the one that someone is glad to see me.

I watched Bran's face brighten when I told him the good news about Nikki.

But after that, when I started telling him what Margaret had told me about his homecoming the summer before last, he seemed to sink back into himself.

When I got to the part about how embarrassing it had been to see how Dr. Zamborska and Tina could hardly keep their hands off each other, he just stared across the room. I looked over at the wall he was staring at to see if I could see what he was seeing, but, of course, I couldn't. Whatever he was seeing was inside his head, and it made him as lonely as his silence. I wished I had skipped that part, but it was too late. You can't unsay what has been said.

To make him feel better (or maybe to make myself feel better) I told him that I was glad he had asked me to talk to Margaret. She had been there. She understood feeling left out, and she helped me understand it, too. As I said that, Branwell had a less faraway look in his eyes. I began to believe that he had chosen Margaret not because she would make him speak but because she would make me understand.

Before I left, I took out the flash cards again and laid them on the table—all except the MARGARET one. The one that got two blinks was THE ANCESTORS.

That was when I was certain that Branwell was not choosing the people who might make him speak. The Ancestors were hardly listener-friendly.

The last time I had spoken to them was when Dr. Z and Tina got married in the university chapel over

Labor Day weekend last year. When he saw me, Mr. Branwell said, "Connor Kane. Good name. You should have gotten Branwell's red hair to go with it." And then he asked me, "Have you met the Russians?" He meant the Zamborska side of the family from Pittsburgh. I didn't know what to say, and I wasn't about to tell him that all of the Zamborskas—including Dr. Zamborska's mother and father—had been born in the United States. Besides, the generation that emigrated came from Ukraine, which wasn't Russia when they emigrated and isn't Russia now either. But I didn't say anything. There was an awful lot that went unsaid when you were with The Ancestors.

When The Ancestors found out that their only grandson was about to have a stepmother whose name was Tina Nguyen and that she was only six years old when she came to America, his grandfather had asked whether she was one of the boat people who had escaped from Vietnam in 1975 after that war. (She was.)

Branwell told The Ancestors that Tina had started school without knowing a word of English and was the Illinois state spelling champion when she was in fourth grade. His grandfather said, "Those Orientals are very good with details."

"What did you say when he said that?" I had asked.

Branwell laughed. "I asked him if he wanted to know what word she won on."

"Did he?"

"He said he did."

"What was it?"

"Molybdenum."

"What did he say when you told him?"

"He said that he wasn't surprised, and when I asked him why, he said, 'Well, now, you know molybdenum is a chemical element. We used it in the automobile industry. There's no getting around it—those Orientals are very good at that sort of thing. Like Tina, a lot of them go into the field of science.'"

"And fingernails," his grandmother had added.

Branwell did not understand what the field of fingernails was, so his grandmother explained that Chrissy, her manicurist, was Vietnamese. "All the people—men as well as woman—who work there are. As a matter of fact, the Vietnamese appear to own fingernail parlors all over Florida. They do good work."

"Of course they do good work," his grandfather had said. "I told you, those Orientals are very good with details."

Then Branwell issued me a challenge. "SIAS attitude of The Ancestors."

I had to think real hard. This is the SIAS I came up with. "Those Orientals will never be *our* Orientals because they have the wrong slant on things."

Bran gave me four stars and wanted to give me five (because, he said, it was subtle), but I told him that we were not going to have grade inflation with our SIAS's.

The Ancestors stayed with Bran for the entire week that Dr. Zamborska and Tina were on their honeymoon. Out of respect for Tina (she said), his grandmother would not allow them to eat with knives and forks. She decided that they must learn to use chopsticks. Actually, Branwell was quite good with them. The Ancestors were not. But they were determined. When Bran held his bowl up close to his face to eat his rice—the way he had seen it done in Chinese restaurants—his grandmother said, "We never allow our bowls to leave the table." And Branwell never told them that *We* may not, but people in Chinese restaurants do.

Branwell would never choose to open up to two people who didn't want to hear that "Orientals" do on occasion allow their bowls to leave the table or that his new stepmother was a superb cook in the French manner. Branwell didn't want to talk to The Ancestors. He wanted me to see them because they, like

Margaret, would help me understand what had happened to him.

I had overheard my parents say that The Ancestors were due in town today with a famous big city lawyer they had hired. I knew that The Ancestors did not change habits easily, so if they were already here, they would be at the motel where they always stayed, which was walking distance from the Behavioral Center.

I decided to try to find them at the motel. If they weren't there, I would leave a message for them, but I hoped I wouldn't have to, because if they called my house, I would have to do more explaining than I wanted to.

(I was beginning to see advantages to being struck dumb.)

They were there. In the motel restaurant. Having the Early Bird supper special. They were surprised to see me. Mr. Branwell invited me to join them, but I told him that my mother was expecting me to have supper at home, so I ordered a Coke and a plate of French fries—something that would hold me but wouldn't spoil my appetite.

After the server brought my order, I told The Ancestors that I had just been to see Branwell, and

Mr. Branwell asked, "So how did you find him?"

"You know that he's not talking."

"Yes," he replied. "We've hired a lawyer—a big city attorney. He's not available until tomorrow afternoon. That's when we'll see our grandson."

I did not know if this attorney came from a big city or if he was a big attorney from a city (big or small) or if *big* meant *best*. Like when a store advertises their biggest sale ever, and they mean their best. I didn't tell them that I didn't think any lawyer—even the biggest—would be able to get Branwell to speak. Especially if they were there when he was.

Instead, I asked them about last summer.

Nikki had been due to arrive in early July, and Bran had told me that he had hoped to be able to skip his visit to The Lovely Condominium—or at least postpone it—but The Ancestors had made it very clear that they expected him for the month. They had booked a cruise of the Caribbean and did not let Bran know about it until all the reservations had been made, and they would have lost their deposit if they canceled.

"We thought it best that Branwell not be around when the new baby arrived," Mr. Branwell said bluntly.

Mrs. Branwell said, "We arranged everything. First-class suite. Top deck. Then we made arrangements to spend a few days in Lauderdale so there would be time to do some shopping for the clothes he would need. We allowed time for the clothes to be altered. He's growing so fast, that boy."

Mr. Branwell continued. "We also engaged a tennis coach for the remainder of the month after we returned from the cruise. But the crucial time—the time that the baby would be born—we would be sailing around the Caribbean, and Branwell wouldn't have to put up with all the commotion of the new baby. I understood that Tina's mother was coming to help her those first couple of weeks."

"Of course," Mrs. Branwell continued, "those Orientals are very family *oriented*." She stopped and laughed nervously. "Of course, Orientals are oriented, but you know what I mean." She laughed nervously again.

Unlike Branwell, I didn't have to be their perfect grandson, so I said, "No, I don't know what you mean, Mrs. Branwell."

"I mean that filling their houses up with lots of relatives is part of their culture. They believe in living under very crowded conditions." Here she looked to her husband for him to agree—which he did by shaking his head.

Then he said, "We just thought that it would be best for Branwell to be away—carefree and cruising the islands—while his house was full of new babies and foreigners. It would not be fair to have him put up with all that confusion. We figured we would keep him until the end of the month as we usually do, and by that time there would be some semblance of normalcy in that house."

Mrs. Branwell smiled patiently. "Or as normal as you can call it with a new baby."

Before he left for his month at The Lovely Condominium, Branwell had shown me a birth announcement that he had designed. It was a drawing of two loosely twisted strands of DNA. He had colored one pink and one blue. He labeled the pink one TINA and the blue one STEFAN. Then the strands got twisted tighter and tighter until it became a line and then an arrow. The arrow pointed to the name NICOLE. Under that, he had written:

DATE OF BIRTH_____

WEIGHT_____

LENGTH _____

*   *   *

Branwell had expected his dad to have his design printed up and sent out to family and friends. But he never told them that. So Tina bought a package of ready-mades and sent those. Dr. Z did fill in the blanks on the one that Branwell had made, and he wrote on the bottom, "She's beautiful, Bran, and she can't wait to meet her brother." He signed it, "Dad and Tina." Tina enclosed a picture of Nikki on which she had written on the back, "Say hello to the incredible Nicole Zamborska, age two days." Dr. Zamborska mailed the announcement and the photo, and they were waiting at The Lovely Condominium when he returned from the cruise of the Caribbean.

Mr. Branwell said, "Branwell couldn't wait to open the envelope. His eyes filled with tears when he saw the announcement and the picture. He wanted to call home immediately, but we"—now it was his turn to look toward his wife to nod in agreement—"we suggested that he wait until he calmed down. After all, we didn't want him crying on the phone and have his father think that we had mistreated him."

I remembered Branwell telling me something, so I asked, "Didn't he ask if he could skip the tennis lessons and go home early?"

Mr. Branwell replied, "Yes. Yes, he did. But we told him that the lessons were paid for in advance. Actually, they were. But the real reason we didn't want to send him home early was because—as I explained—we didn't know how he would fit in to that crowd with the new baby and that mother-in-law in the house. Cooking up all that rice and baby formula. We thought it best that he stay with us."

Mrs. Branwell nodded. "It was the right decision."

I asked, "Were you surprised to find out that Tina and Dr. Zamborska had hired someone to help take care of Nikki?"

Mr. Branwell said, "Yes, we were. But we knew that Tina would not be a stay-at-home mom. Those Orientals are very ambitious, you know. Especially the immigrants."

That's when I thanked them for the French fries and excused myself. I reached across the table to shake their hands and, as I shook Mrs. Branwell's, I said, "Nice nails."

She hurriedly withdrew her hand from mine, blushed, and said, "Thank you."

6.

When I got home from my meeting with The Ancestors, I called Dr. Zamborska and told him that I would like to be there when Branwell met with them and the lawyer they had hired, whose name I found out was Neville Beacham.

Since Branwell was only allowed to have two visitors at a time, I would need special permission to be allowed to see him at the same time as one of The Ancestors and Beacham. I suggested to him that I should be allowed to go in as an interpreter just as the hearing impaired have an interpreter doing sign language. I didn't want to reveal to him my means of communicating with Branwell (I don't know why), but I knew that I would if I had to.

As it turned out I didn't have to.

I think the fact that The Ancestors had not bothered to consult with Dr. Zamborska about hiring another attorney and the fact that they obviously didn't want him there helped convince him that I should be a third—or fourth—person present. He agreed to call and request permission. And then I told him my other problem: I couldn't be at the Behavioral Center until school was out, which would make it necessary for The Ancestors to change the time of their appointment. I think Dr. Z was enjoying putting up obstacles for them.

I don't know how he did it—except that he is a lot more competent than he appears to be. Early the next morning before I left for school, he called to tell me that he had made it happen.

Dr. Z left it to me to call The Ancestors at their motel to tell them that their time to visit Branwell had been changed. Mrs. Branwell answered the phone, and I could tell she did not want to believe me or believe that I had the right to be telling her in the first place. I told her that she better believe me or she would get to the Behavioral Center and find out that she and Mr. Branwell and the attorney they had hired couldn't get in. She said, "Perhaps you better explain this to Mr. Branwell."

He was even less accustomed than his wife to having someone my age tell him to change his plans. He said that he would call the Center to get the facts. I mentioned that the offices at the Center were closed now, and I suggested that he call at nine when they would be open. He sputtered on his end of the phone, which I interpreted to mean that he did not approve, so I said, "See you at four," and I hung up.

I had to do all that before I caught the bus for school, but this was Thursday, and Thursday has always been my lucky day.

When the guard at the desk did her usual search, she pulled my flash cards out and jerked her head toward The Ancestors and Beacham. I gave her a minimal shake of my head. She smiled knowingly and quietly dropped them into my backpack.

The Big City Lawyer turned out to be a man of average height with a Hollywood hairstyle and a capped-tooth smile the likes of which I had only seen on one person—a TV evangelist. He was from Detroit. I may be interpreting (what else did I have to go on?), but I did think Branwell looked relieved when he saw us enter alphabetically: Ancestors, Beacham, Connor.

Since I had been coming to the Behavioral Center, Branwell and I were developing a new kind of understanding. I know this will sound funny, but I've thought about it a lot, and I don't mean it in any negative way. The relationship that Branwell and I were developing was something like that between a boy and his dog. This is the way I mean it: For one thing, we had developed a means of communication that was verbal on only one side. I could speak; he couldn't. But it wasn't just that. Branwell had become dependent on me for his contact with the outside world. And it wasn't just that either. It was also that I had developed a dependence on him for needing me. He needed me, and I needed him to need me. That's what I mean about a boy and his dog—nice, like that.

Even though Branwell did not speak a word during the whole meeting, he said a lot, and as things turned out, it was a good thing—a very good thing—that I was there.

It was almost comical to see Big Beacham try and try again to get Branwell to talk. When Branwell would not even make eye contact with him, he spoke louder and louder. Even Mr. Branwell realized how wrong this technique was, because he turned his back to me, cupped his mouth with his hand, and whispered something directly into the attorney's ear. They looked at me. After all, I was there as Branwell's interpreter, but I was not about to reveal my technique for communicating with him. I shrugged and held my hands out, palms up, in a gesture of helplessness. At that point, the attorney took a little cassette player out of his briefcase and played the 911 tape.

Operator: *Epiphany 911. Hobson speaking.*
SILENCE.
Operator: *Epiphany 911. Hobson. May I help you?*
SILENCE. [Voices are heard in the background.]
Operator: *Anyone there?*
A woman's voice [screaming in the background]: *Tell them. Tell them.*
Operator: *Ma'am, I can't hear you.* [then louder] *Please come to the phone.*
A woman's voice [still in the background, but louder now]: *Tell them.* [then, screaming as the voice approaches] *For God's sake, Branwell.* [the voice gets louder] *TELL THEM.*
SILENCE.
Operator: *Please speak into the phone.*
A woman's voice [heard more clearly]: *TELL THEM. NOW BRAN. TELL THEM NOW.*

SILENCE.

<u>A woman's voice with a British accent</u> [heard clearly]: *Here! Take her! For God's sake, at least take her!* [then speaking directly into the phone] *It's the baby. She won't wake up.*

<u>Operator</u>: *Stay on the phone.*

<u>British Accent</u> [frightened]: *The baby won't wake up.*

<u>Operator</u>: *Stay on the line. We're transferring you to Fire and Rescue.*

<u>Male Voice</u>: *Epiphany Fire and Rescue. Davidson. What is the nature of your emergency?*

<u>British Accent</u>: *The baby won't wake up.*

<u>Male Voice</u>: *What is your exact location?*

<u>British Accent</u>: *198 Tower Hill Road. Help, please. It's the baby.*

<u>Male Voice</u>: *Help is on the way, ma'am. What happened?*

<u>British Accent</u>: *He dropped her. She won't wake up.*

<u>Male Voice</u>: *Is she having difficulty breathing?*

<u>British Accent</u> [panicky now]: *Yes. Her breathing is all strange.*

<u>Male Voice</u>: *How old is the baby, ma'am?*

<u>British Accent</u>: *Almost six months.*

<u>Male Voice</u>: *Is there a history of asthma or heart trouble?*

<u>British Accent</u>: *No, no. He dropped her, I tell you.*

LOUD BANGING IS HEARD.

<u>British Accent</u> [into the phone]: *They're here. Thank God. They're here.* [then just before the connection is broken] *For God's sake, Branwell, MOVE. Open the door.*

Funny thing: As the tape was playing, the grown-ups watched the tape. When given a choice, people will always watch something that moves—even if it's only the tiny wheels of a cassette player. But I watched Branwell. He sat perfectly still, his hands folded on the table in front of him. When the tape got to the part where the operator says that she is transferring the call to Fire and Rescue, Branwell squinted his eyes and moved his clenched fist in front of his mouth.

The two men paid no attention to me at all. Which was good. It allowed me to be silent and to listen. I didn't just listen, I fine-tuned my listener. And I watched. The energy I would normally use for thinking up what I was going to say went into listening hard and watching well, and I remembered everything.

I listened like Branwell, struck dumb.

Think of it this way. Think that you're in a restaurant. You're in a restaurant, and the server comes to the table to recite the specials of the day. Most of the time you only half-listen because (1) you want to hear it all before you make your choice and (2) after you have chosen, you know you can always ask, "What did you say comes with the *osso buco?*" But if you have to listen as Branwell would—as if you could not speak, could not ask—you would have to remember what comes with the *osso buco* and make your choice without asking.

That meeting with the irritating, aggravating, annoying Ancestors and Big Beacham made me glad that Branwell could not speak. Not speaking was the only weapon he had. Branwell knew all the choices on the menu, and for once, he wasn't taking the *risotto* just because it came with the *osso buco.*

7.

I called Dr. Zamborska from Margaret's and reported on the meeting. When I described their lack of success in getting Branwell to speak, there was a long silence on his end of the line. As much as Dr. Z wanted his son to speak, that long pause on his end of the line told me that he was glad that Branwell didn't do it for The Ancestors. I was learning that silence can say a lot.

I still had not told even Dr. Zamborska that I had found a way to communicate with Bran, and I still was not sure why. Maybe I wanted a monopoly. Maybe—and believe this of me if you are kind—I didn't think Branwell would want me to.

But I knew there was something on the tape that Branwell wanted me to investigate.

I knew where the spot was—the part where the operator said that she was transferring the call to Fire and Rescue and the part where Epiphany Fire and Rescue comes on. That's when Branwell squinted his eyes and moved his clenched fist in front of his mouth. I knew where it was, but I was not sure what it was. I also did not know how I would get a copy of it to take to him so that we could go over it.

I told Margaret about the session with The Ancestors and the tape and asked her if we could get a copy. She said that it shouldn't be too hard to get, because the tape was part of the public record. "Let's call the Communications Center. They should release a copy if we need it for a possible defense."

"Just what is Branwell being defended against?"

Margaret said, "Sit down, Connor." I did. "He can be charged with aggravated assault . . . or . . . worse. Depending on what happens to Nikki."

"Nikki? Nikki's going to be all right, isn't she? She's already opened her eyes."

"Connor," Margaret said gently, "Nikki is not out of the woods. Technically, she's out of the coma, and they are weaning her off the respirator, but she is now entering what they call Stage Three. It can last a few days or a week or a month or many, many months."

"But eventually, she'll be all right, won't she?"

"I don't know, Connor. No one does. Everything about the outcome is still iffy. It's a cruel time."

"So if something bad—really bad—I mean *really* bad, like the worst possible thing—happens to Nikki, what will happen to Bran?"

"Manslaughter. He'll be charged with manslaughter if he did not hurt her deliberately. But if they can prove otherwise—that he hurt her on purpose—he'll be charged with murder."

I panicked. "They have no right to charge him. He didn't hurt that baby," I said.

"Did he tell you that?" Margaret asked.

"You know he didn't. He's not speaking. That's what I'm trying to do. I'm trying to get him to speak. The tape," I said. "We need to get a copy of that tape."

Margaret sensed my panic. In a voice as calming as a lullaby, she said, "Let me make a few calls and see if we can get a copy."

She went back to her office to make the calls, and I sat there trying to calm myself down. I needed to find out what had made Branwell stop talking if I was going to find a way to make him start. But if I was going to help him—really, really help him—I had to find out what had happened on the day of the 911 call.

I don't know who Margaret talked to or what she said, but when she got off the phone, she told me that she would be picking up the tape the following afternoon.

"What do you think is wrong with Branwell?" I asked.

"I think he's afraid."

"Of what?"

Margaret smiled. "I don't know, Connor. I really don't. Do you want to talk about it?"

I nodded.

We sat on opposite ends of the sofa in the add-on living room. Margaret tucked her legs up under her and asked, "What do you know of Branwell's reaction to Tina?"

Why was she starting there? That was like going to the doctor's office for a pain in your stomach and he starts by taking your blood pressure in your arm. I told her that Branwell had never said much about Tina except to say that he had never seen his father so crazy about anyone. When I reminded him what my mother had said about his father's coming into the nursery to give him his bottles while the other mothers were nursing their babies, he blushed. "Yeah," he had said, "I can't complain. Don't get me wrong. I know my father loves me. But the way my father loves Tina is different. The way a man loves a woman is different from the way a father loves a son."

Once, before they got married, I had asked him if he liked Tina, and he had said, "Yes. Yes, I do. I don't love her the way my father does. I don't know if I love her at all. But I do like her. Do you think that's enough?"

No one had ever asked me that before, so I told him that my father always says that it's as important for a parent to like his children as it is for him to love them. Then I added, "I'm not sure that love and like aren't like cats and dogs: One can't grow up to be the other, but they can be taught to live under the same roof."

Branwell had clapped his hand on my shoulder. (When Branwell clapped a friendly hand on your shoulder, it was always something between a slap and a clamp. Sometimes his movements were so heavy, you wanted to poke him back.) "You always give me something to think about, pal."

"You like that in me, eh?"

"*Like,* yeah, but don't call it love."

Margaret moved from taking blood pressure to taking temperature. She asked me about Branwell's reaction to Nikki. I told her what I knew.

The baby was born on the Fourth of July. She was over three weeks old when The Ancestors finally released Branwell from The Lovely Condominium. Tina and Dr. Zamborska and Nikki were all there to meet his plane. Bran was still an unaccompanied minor, so he had to wait until his father showed proper ID before he could go over to where Tina was holding the baby. In Florida he had bought a mobile of natural seashells for above the baby's crib, and he was so excited and suddenly so shy about at last seeing his baby sister that he awkwardly thrust the package at Tina and said, "Here." What he had wanted was for her to take the package so that he could take the baby, but Tina stepped back and the package fell to the floor. He bent down to pick it up and in a rush of words said, "I wanted to get something that doesn't take any batteries, but there is some assembly required. But it's all natural. Even the string. Well, maybe not the string. The string may be nylon, and nylon isn't natural. The Ancestors sent something, too. It's clothes. Packed in my suitcase. I'll unpack it when we get to the house."

Branwell told me that he had read somewhere that schools that were trying to keep teenagers from having babies had made them carry a five-pound sack of flour around with them all day, and he had been practicing holding the baby by holding a sack of flour. Actually, he had been practicing in secret because The Ancestors had cautioned him, "We don't want you to become a servant to that child. You are not to be a volunteer baby-sitter, Branwell. You are not to make yourself available whenever Tina wants."

Considering the way that Branwell had practically fallen over himself, Tina didn't volunteer to hand Nikki over to Branwell. Instead, she clutched her closer before pulling the little blanket back from her face so that Bran could get a better look. He leaned forward toward Nikki and studied her. "Well, what do you think?" Dr. Zamborska asked. "What is your first impression of your baby sister?"

"Half sister," he replied.

Margaret asked, "Could Branwell explain why he said that?"

"Never could. Did you say something like that when you saw me for the first time? Did you say, 'half brother'?"

Margaret laughed. "I don't think I said it. But I probably thought it." She waited a minute before adding, "I guess that remark along with the fact that he never asked to hold Nikki—"

"He didn't know that he should have."

"Of course he didn't. But Tina didn't know that. Branwell gave the impression that he was staking out his place in the family, letting them know that he was there first." Margaret sipped her cider and said, "I'm sure that Branwell's long stay in Florida—even though it was not his choice—along with that *half sister* remark, along with not taking the baby gave Dr. Zamborska and Tina the impression that he was jealous."

"But he wasn't. He told me that he thought she was beautiful."

"You know, Connor," she said, "first impressions—especially when everyone is watching and waiting, looking for signs—are hard to overcome."

"Is that why you've never liked my mother?"

Margaret thought awhile before she answered. "Maybe." Margaret was too honest a person to ever deny that she did not like my mother. "But it was The Registrar that I most changed my mind about. He is not the father I thought he was."

"He likes you, Margaret. He always says that it's as important for a parent to like his children as it is for him to love them."

"The Registrar says that, does he?"

"Often."

"Yeah," she said, "he has a way with animals."

I drank the rest of my cider and set my glass down. "I guess I'll be getting back."

"Would you like me to drive you?"

"I thought you'd never ask."

Margaret smiled. "I have another thought. Why don't you stay for supper? Vivian is back in town, and Gretchen Silver wants to see her before she leaves."

"Where has she been?"

"According to her contract, Vivian was entitled to two weeks' vacation after she finished her year with the Zamborskas. Under the circumstances, she fulfilled only one fourth of her contract, but Tina and Dr. Z gave her one week—half her due. She just got back from wherever it was she went."

"Where is she now, and where is she going?"

"She is now at the Holiday Inn, and I don't know where she's going, but my guess would be that she's going to her next job assignment. I was going to pick her up at the motel and bring her over here for dinner. Want to join us?"

I said yes immediately. This was an offer I couldn't refuse. Vivian had been Nikki's nanny. Actually, she was an *au pair*. (There's a difference.) Hers was the British accent on the 911 tape.

Margaret said, "Call your mother and tell her you're having dinner at The Evil Empire."

"Why do you say that, Margaret? My mother likes you."

"It is convenient for her to like me."

"And maybe it's convenient for you to hate her."

"Let me think about that one," she said. "Now, do you want to call your mother or not?"

"Want to."

I started for the phone, and Margaret said, "You know, Connor, kids who grow up in a university develop smart mouths before their brains can catch up."

"You grew up in a university, too, remember."

"That's my point."

I made the call but did not tell my mother that Vivian was coming over. Margaret was putting on a jacket when I hung up. "Well," she said, "am I dropping you home on my way to the motel? Or are you staying?"

"Staying." She started out the back door. "Before you go, do you mind telling me why Gretchen Silver wants to see Vivian?"

"She's giving a deposition to the prosecution."

"Oh."

I know I looked puzzled, for instead of leaving, Margaret closed the door and asked, "Do you know what a deposition is?" I shrugged. *Deposition* was one of those words that you always think you know the meaning of until you are asked to define it. "A deposition," Margaret said, "is a statement by a witness that is written down or recorded for use in court at a later date."

"Is Branwell really being prosecuted?"

"Let's say they're gathering information."

I felt my blood go cold—or at least drain from my face. Margaret put a hand on my shoulder. "Are you all right?" My throat was so dry, I couldn't speak. I just nodded yes. "It's not a game, after all, is it, Connor?" I shook my head no. I didn't bother telling her that I had come to that same conclusion just about a half hour ago. "Why don't you set the table while I'm gone. Wineglasses for Vivian and me. Coke glass for you. You know where everything is."

8.

After I finished setting the table, I took one of the spare cards and wrote TAPE. I stacked the cards and bound them with a rubber band, leaving TAPE on top.

I took dishes down from the cupboard and silverware from the drawer and set the table. I thought about Vivian. And Branwell. And Branwell with Vivian. And how my friendship with Branwell changed after Vivian Shawcurt arrived at 198 Tower Hill Road.

It all started on our way to the bus stop the first day of school. We had hardly seen each other over the summer, and the first words out of his mouth were, "Our au pair has arrived from England."

I had never heard of an *awe pear* before, and Branwell was not volunteering any more information, and there was something about his tone of voice that put me off, so I was not about to ask what an *awe pear* was. When I tried to look it up, I couldn't because *awe* is in the dictionary and so is *pear,* but *awe pear* is not *au pair.* Somehow, I found out how to spell it and looked it up, and I was a little bit puzzled because the dictionary said that an *au pair* is a young foreigner who works for a family in exchange for room and board and a chance to learn the family's language. Branwell had said that their *au pair* was coming from England, and although I have never been there to hear it for myself, I very well knew that people in England spoke English but with an accent.

I asked my father about au pairs. He knew all about them. Being the registrar at the university, he has to know a lot about people coming from England and other places. Au pairs frequently work for university families because they are encouraged to take educational courses during their exchange year.

The Zamborskas were expected to treat Vivian more like a family member than like an employee. They were supposed to include her in family celebrations and vacations and help her enroll in educational programs and even pay her tuition if necessary. They had to give her a private room and all her meals, $140 a week for pocket money, and at least once a month she was to have off one full weekend—from Friday evening until Monday morning. If they needed her to baby-sit on Saturday nights or any other nights, she was supposed to be paid extra or given more time off during the week.

In exchange, the au pair was to help out with child care for up to forty-five hours per week, five and one half days per week. She was supposed to have no more than six hours of active duty (such as feeding, bathing, and playing with the children) a day and three hours of "passive availability"—meaning that she baby-sits while the children sleep, play by themselves, or watch TV. Those hours of passive availability are considered part of the forty-five hours of child care she would owe the Zamborskas.

Vivian Shawcurt was twenty years old but looked like a teenager—of which she was only one year on the far side of. She was only five feet two inches tall. And although Branwell had just entered his teens, he towered over her.

Because of his love of words, in a strange way, it was the language difference—*English* English versus *American* English—that started Branwell's fascination with the au pair. He fell in love with her British accent, and at first he couldn't stop talking about her. He referred to her as Vivi and told me that she had asked him to call her that.

Halfway between Tower Hill Road and Margaret's, in the middle of the campus, there is a suspension bridge over a deep gorge that had been carved out by the glaciers. The walls of the gorge form a bowl, and water falls over the edge onto the rocky bottom of a creek below. Everyone calls the gorge The Ditch. There is a zigzag path down to the bottom, and when the weather is good, the trail is full of hikers and joggers. After the trees leaf out, young lovers often hide in the shadows of the trail.

The bridge over the gorge is only wide enough for two people to walk side by side. It is a popular meeting place. If you say to someone, "Meet me over The Ditch," they know you mean the bridge over the gorge.

When Branwell and I were little, we used to stand on the bridge over the gorge and look for lovers on the path to the bottom.

One day in early September shortly after Vivian had arrived, Branwell and I were on our way to the campus bookstore to get our school supplies, and we stopped on the bridge and looked down. The trees were still in full leaf, and we couldn't spot any lovers, so Branwell rested his arms on the bridge railing and spoke to the open air. "She calls gasoline *petrol*. A motorcycle is a *motorbike* and a truck, a *lorry*."And then he looked at me with an other-worldly smile.

I knew he was talking about Vivian, but I pretended that I didn't. "Who?" I asked.

"Oh?" he said, surprised. "Vivian Shawcurt. Our English au pair."

"And what would she call the goofy look you have on your face?" I asked. Branwell blushed. He turned away from The Ditch and looked at me, puzzled. My sarcasm surprised me as much as it surprised him. Something in his dreamy look had set me off.

He said nothing more, and neither did I.

I was never in their company very much, but one time I heard her call him Brannie. No one else ever called him that. He hated it, and let everyone know he did. I have already mentioned how kids at school didn't mess with Branwell. There was something about him—maybe it was his brains or his sincerity—*something* kept kids from messing with him. So once he let someone know he didn't like being called Brannie, they didn't. Except Vivi. I heard her call him that, and I didn't hear him correct her. When I heard her call him that, I knew that there was something special between them that I was not to be part of.

After a while, Bran stopped talking about her, and our friendship changed. By the middle of October, Branwell hardly had time for me at all. He rushed home from school every day. I assumed that he had chosen to spend his after-school hours with her instead of me.

Dr. Zamborska and Tina were loose about how Vivian spent her time when they were home and she was off duty. The city bus stop for Tower Hill Road is right across the street from my house, and on the evenings when I wandered over to the window after supper, I would see her out there, ready to catch the eight o'clock bus to town. Even when it was not real cold, she wore a cranberry red hat that she pulled down over her ears. The hat had two tassels on a knitted string that bounced as she stepped up onto the bus.

On Veterans Day, November 11, which was on a Wednesday, Bran and I had the day off from school. Bran was supposed to come to my house at noon, and my mother was to take us to lunch at Ruby Tuesdays. Then we were to go to the multiplex while my mother "picked up a few things at the mall," which is what she calls shopping. It had been a month since we had spent a whole afternoon together. At eleven that morning, the phone rang. I was expecting it to be Bran, saying, "Blue peter." I smiled as I picked up the phone, thinking that I was going to tell him that we were on Eastern Standard Time now and had been for more than a week and that noon was still an hour away. (I couldn't believe that I was actually rehearsing what I would say to him.)

It was Bran, all right, but he was not saying, "Blue peter." He was whispering into the phone. "Listen, Connor," he said, "I won't be able to make it today."

"What's the matter with you, Bran? Speak up."

"I can't."

"Why not?"

"I can't because . . . because I have a sore throat, that's why."

I didn't believe for one minute that he had a sore throat. "Are you telling me that Brannie wants to stay home and play patient with Nurse Vivi?"

"Nothing like that," he whispered. "Cut it out."

I couldn't stand the whispering. "Speak up, Bran," I said.

He hung up.

* * *

I had written VIVIAN on one of the flash cards. I would have predicted that she would be one of the first that Branwell would blink at. But when he didn't, I thought it was because he had never wanted to share her with me.

I was glad that Margaret had asked me to stay for supper.

9.

When she walked in with Vivian, Margaret said, "You remember Vivian Shawcurt, don't you, Connor?"

"Sure," I said.

Vivian handed Margaret a small pot of African violets. The pot was covered with shiny pink paper that made a cuff around the lip. "Thank you for having me over to dinner," she said.

Margaret took the flowers and said, "Thanks." Then, turning to me, she said, "Connor, why don't you put these on the table as a centerpiece?" As I took the flowers from her, I thought that she should have said something more. Like how pretty the flowers were or how thoughtful it was of Vivian to bring them. But she didn't. She said, "You've met my brother, haven't you?"

Vivian replied, "You're Connor, Branwell's good friend, aren't you?" I said that I was. "How's he doing?" she asked.

I didn't know how to answer that. I had to say something, but I didn't know what, and that became probably the seventh time since Branwell went silent that I wished that I was, too, because the truth is that if you don't say anything, you can't say anything wrong. The best I could come up with was, "All right, I guess."

Vivian took off her coat. She was wearing a short plaid skirt, black stockings, and a pale blue sweater that looked as soft as a baby blanket. I remembered that Branwell had told me that she called pullover sweaters *jumpers*. (That is, when he was still talking about her to me.)

She took off her tasseled hat. Her hair was blond, parted in the middle, and twisted into a roll on either side. The two rolls were held together in the back with a plastic barrette. The strands that were held in the barrette were a lighter shade than the rest. Her hair looked the way I had always imagined a skein of flax spun into gold by the miller's daughter would. I remembered that Branwell had told me that she called barrettes *hair grips*.

Vivian herself looked like one of those English

schoolgirls you see on TV. Except her outfit did not look like a school uniform—or at least that blue jumper didn't. She definitely was an older woman, and as soon as she took off her coat and tasseled hat, I could understand how Branwell might have gotten interested in jumpers and hair grips and not just because they were the *English* English names of things.

Margaret looked at the pot of violets I was holding and jerked her head toward the kitchen. Margaret can be bossy like that, and I didn't appreciate her ordering me around, even if she did it silently. I silently disobeyed. I stayed put until Vivian looked comfortably seated on the far end of the sofa. Then I said, in a grown-up voice, "Will you excuse me a minute?" And with a cold look at Margaret—who smiled in return— I went into the kitchen and put the pot of violets on the table.

I heard Margaret ask, "White or red?" She was referring to wine.

Vivian answered, "Whichever you're having."

As Margaret and I passed each other at the kitchen door, under her breath, she said, "Watch your head." I looked up. I wasn't about to bump my head on anything. It wasn't until much later that I knew what she meant.

When I returned to the living room, I sat down on the chair that was opposite the end of the sofa where Vivian was seated. She fastened her bright blue eyes on me and said, "Margaret told me that you've been to see him."

"Branwell?" I asked. "Do you mean Branwell?" She nodded. "Yes, I've seen him."

Vivian did not have a chance to ask me anything else because Margaret appeared carrying two glasses of red wine. She handed one to Vivian and said, "Your Coke's chilling in the fridge, Connor. Want to help yourself and join us?" I thought that the least Margaret could have done would be to bring me my Coke. When my back was to Vivian, I passed her a smoldering look as I made my way back into the kitchen. I slammed the refrigerator door after taking out my Coke. I decided to wrap the can in a napkin—mostly so that I could slam the napkin drawer when I shut it. I wanted to say something grown-up, possibly something memorable, so when I returned to the living room, I said, "I would like to make a toast."

"Fine," Margaret said, smiling and lifting an eyebrow in the way she does when she is secretly amused. "What wouldst thou propose?" she asked sarcastically.

I lifted my glass and said, "To Nicole Zamborska, Nikki."

Margaret's smile went from sarcastic to sincere. "That was very thoughtful, Connor. Poor little Nikki seems to be the forgotten soul in all of this."

Vivian held her glass high, lowered it, took a dainty sip, and replied, "Such a sweet child, was Nikki. I never thought that Brannie would do anything to hurt her. He was always so . . . so . . . interested in her. Of course, I sometimes wondered . . ." Vivian laid her wineglass down on the coffee table and took a small handful of peanuts in her right hand. She opened her hand and studied the peanuts for what seemed like a minute before choosing one. She held it between her thumb and forefinger, suspended between her lap and her mouth.

"Wondered what?" Margaret asked.

Vivian continued studying that peanut before looking directly at Margaret. "I sometimes wondered if he wasn't a little *too* interested in his little sister."

"What do you mean by that?" Margaret asked bluntly.

Vivian at last put the peanut in her mouth and chewed on it long enough for it to have been the whole handful. She swallowed. (I did, too, even though I wasn't eating peanuts.) "I just wondered if Brannie would have been as interested in the baby if *Nikki* had been short for *Nicholas* instead of *Nicole*."

"You better explain," Margaret said.

Vivian looked from me to Margaret and back to me. Finally she said, "Connor, did Branwell ever tell you about what happened the first week I worked there?"

I shook my head no.

"Are you sure?"

I didn't know whether to shake my head no that he didn't tell me or to nod my head yes, that I was sure. So I said, "He never said much about you."

"Well, that doesn't surprise me. I suppose he had to keep his little secrets."

I waited while Vivian put another peanut in her mouth and chewed it endlessly. Finally, she smiled (slowly) and said, "Well, I might as well tell you. I am about to be deposed, you know, and I shall have to tell them, shan't I?" She took a lengthy sip of wine.

Without being asked, Margaret lifted the bottle, raised it to the rim of Vivian's glass, and poured in a single motion. Then Margaret leaned back into the sofa and folded her hands over her stomach. She was as anxious to hear what Vivian had to say as I was, and Vivian knew her time was up. She drew a deep breath and began. "Do you know what a Jack-and-Jill bathroom is?" she asked.

Margaret swept her hand around the room. "The houses in Old Town," she said, "were built when a family of five or seven or ten all shared the same bathroom. When I was eleven years old, I lived here one summer with two great-uncles, and the single upstairs bathroom served both those Jacks and this Jill."

Vivian laughed. "Actually, that is true of where I live in England as well. I had never before heard of a Jack-and-Jill bathroom until I came to the States. What it means is a bathroom that is between two bedrooms and has a door from each of those bedrooms into the bath. But there is no entry from the hall. It was Brannie himself who told me that they were called Jack-and-Jill. He loved having the proper names of things, Brannie did."

"Still does," Margaret corrected.

"Has he spoken?" Vivian asked.

"No, but he also has not died, so I assume he still loves having the proper names of things even if he isn't saying them."

I cleared my throat to get attention. I said, "You were telling us about the Jack-and-Jill bathroom."

"Yes, so I was." She tilted the wineglass back only

enough to wet her lips. "Well, when I arrived at the Zamborskas', they gave me what had been the guest bedroom and converted what had been Branwell's bedroom into the nursery. That way, I could connect easily to the nursery through the bathroom. My bedroom opened onto the toilet side of the Jack-and-Jill, and the nursery opened onto the bathtub end. Both bedrooms—but not the bathroom—also have doors from the upstairs hall. Branwell was moved downstairs to the bedroom that was off the kitchen. I understand that in many American homes, this is called 'the mother-in-law suite,' and that is where an au pair would normally sleep. But since Nikki was so young and was still often waking at night, the Zamborskas decided that it would be best to have me in the guest bedroom that was on one side of the Jack-and-Jill, and have Nikki in the nursery on the other."

Now that she had laid out the geography of the bedrooms and the bathrooms, Vivian took another drink of wine and drained her glass. Without being asked, Margaret filled it up again.

"Actually, we Brits like a proper bath, you know. I say showers are not nearly as therapeutic. The first week I was there, I had just submerged, ready to settle in for a good soak, when what should happen but that the door at the nursery end of the bathroom opens. I whipped my head around, called out, 'Hello? Hello?' and who should I see there but Branwell. He stopped dead in his tracks and turned as red as his hair before muttering, 'Sorry' and walking out."

Margaret said, "Don't you think that was quite a natural mistake? After all, he was coming in from what—until only a short time ago—had been his bedroom."

"That is true. And I find that a perfectly logical reason for something like that to happen once." Vivian plucked a single peanut from the bowl and held it between her thumb and forefinger and studied it for a while. When she took her eyes off the peanut she looked from Margaret to me and asked, "How do you explain its happening twice?" She seemed to be waiting for an answer. Most particularly from me. It was me she was looking at now. Not until Margaret cleared her throat did she look away.

"Last year," Margaret began, "yes, it was just about a year ago, I changed around my kitchen drawers. I put the silverware where the napkins were, and I put the napkins where the dish towels were. Do you know what? Even last week I was still reaching into the wrong drawer for the silverware."

Vivian put that peanut—no, *placed* that peanut—on

her tongue and slowly closed her lips. She just stared into space, and then, shaking her head sadly, asked, "Can you explain its happening a third time?"

There was dead silence in the room.

Vivian looked first to Margaret and then to me for an answer. We had none. She reached for her pocketbook, opened it, and took out a pack of cigarettes. She offered one to Margaret, who refused, and started searching for something inside her pocketbook. She didn't find what she wanted, so she turned to me and asked, "Connor, would you please get me a light?" Margaret does not smoke and does not approve of smoking, so I didn't look at Margaret for permission to get Vivian a match. There was a packet of them on the kitchen countertop that Margaret had put there so that she could light the candles on the table.

I started to hand Vivian the packet, but instead of taking it, she put the cigarette between her lips and leaned forward. I assumed she wanted me to light it for her. (I had seen that sort of thing in the movies.) So I tried to strike the match, but I was not successful. I had never before lit a match. We had an electric stove, and on the rare occasions when we ate by candlelight, my mother lit them, and when the charcoal grill was to be lit, my dad did that. No one in my family smoked. Firecrackers were illegal. When would I ever have had a chance to practice lighting matches? I closed the cover before striking, but the cardboard of the matches kept bending on me. Finally, I held one close enough to the head of the match to get it to take, and Vivian leaned forward with the cigarette between her lips. She held my wrist that held the match until she had sucked in enough fire for the entire end of her cigarette to catch. Before she let go of my wrist, she looked up at me and said, "Thank you, Connor. You are a gentleman."

Just like in the movies.

At that moment, I knew why no one should be allowed to play with matches. There's no telling what besides a cigarette may catch fire.

Vivian looked around for an ashtray but couldn't find one. (There's not a single one in the house. As I said, Margaret does not approve of smoking, but she believes a lot in personal choice, so she would never forbid someone from doing it.) Vivian said, "Margaret, may I use a saucer for an ashtray?"

Margaret didn't exactly say yes. She said, "Connor, would you please bring Vivian a saucer?" I nodded yes but forgot to move. I watched as Vivian took a long drag on her cigarette, pursed her lips as if blowing kisses, and blew out the smoke. I watched until the last faint puff of smoke disappeared.

Vivian said, "Connor? A saucer?"

"Oh, yes," I said. "Yes. Yes, of course." If she had asked me for a flying saucer, I would have sprouted wings and searched the night sky for one.

As I walked back toward the kitchen, I heard Vivian say, "Actually, there's more."

"About Branwell?"

"Yes."

"What about him?"

"About his interests, actually." Vivian was speaking slightly above a whisper, but Margaret's kitchen is right next to the add-on living room, so I could hear practically everything.

Margaret spoke in a normal voice. "Will this be something you will be saying at your deposition?"

Vivian replied, "I'm afraid I will have to, won't I?"

"I suppose so," Margaret said.

Then I heard, ". . . unhealthy interest . . . nappies."

Nappies are what the British call diapers. The word had amused Branwell. He told me that it came from napkins. "When you think about it, Con," he had said, "diapers do the same thing that napkins do. They catch a mess." After Vivian arrived on Tower Hill Road,

Branwell had also started calling the toilet the *loo.* He did that with me, but not with other kids. He knew exactly where they drew the line between *different* and *weird,* and he never crossed it.

"Actually," Vivian said, "I'm not sure this is the right time."

I took a saucer from the cabinet and returned to the living room as Margaret was saying, "Actually, Vivian, this is a very good time. Think of it as a dress rehearsal for the lawyers."

Vivian topped off her glass of wine, settled back into her chair, and said, "I don't know how to put this delicately."

"Then try directly," Margaret said.

"All right, then," she said, setting her glass down firmly on the coffee table. "Here goes. Branwell Zamborska seemed to have an unhealthy interest in little Nikki's nappies." Still holding her cigarette between her first two fingers, she leaned forward and picked up her wineglass in her cigarette-holding hand. Peering mischievously at me over the rim, she said, "Of course, a lot of it was little-boy curiosity, you know."

Margaret asked, "What do you mean?"

"Oh, you know. A little boy's curiosity about what the other sex keeps inside her panties."

Margaret looked over at me to see how I was taking this information. I was doing all right even though I had never had a discussion about sex with a mature woman before.

Margaret said, "Don't you think it's a natural curiosity? I remember when Connor here was a baby, I actually asked to change his nappy. Once."

Vivian asked, "Did you, really?"

"Yes. When he was new, and I was young and curious."

Laughing, Vivian said, "What did you find out?"

Margaret looked at me and smiled. "That God has a sense of humor after all." I flared my nostrils at her and jerked my head away. I should have stayed in the kitchen.

Vivian said, "At first I thought it was only the natural curiosity of a thirteen-year-old boy. But after awhile, it became something else. Branwell became absolutely obsessive about changing Nikki's nappies. That *wasn't* . . . wasn't . . . *natural* . . . " Her voice trailed off as if she had ended that sentence with a comma and not a period. She transferred her wineglass to her other hand and took a long drag on her cigarette before saying, "It seemed to me that Brannie always spread the cheeks of her little bum and spread her little legs and wiped and wiped some more. All that wiping. All that powdering . . ."

Margaret said, "On the rare occasion when I was requested to change Connor's nappy, his mother always insisted that I clean all his little bits and pieces." Margaret was determined to embarrass me. She was pissing me off. "Even though there wasn't that much to do," she said, smiling—she was really pissing me off—"the whole process was nothing but a chore." Really, really pissing me off.

Vivian said, "I kept thinking that Branwell, too, would find it a chore and just stop, but he didn't. Even when I was there, he insisted on changing her nappies himself."

At last I knew why Branwell rushed home from school every day.

"I tell you, he was always changing her. Whether she needed it or not." She took a long pull on her cigarette. I held my breath as I watched the ash grow until it seemed ready to drop. But as she took it from her mouth, she held it straight until it was over the saucer. With the tiniest flick of her finger, she made the ash drop. Then with a delicate movement of her wrist, she stubbed it out. "Actually," she said, "I think that's when he did it."

"Did what?" Margaret asked.

Vivian answered in a hoarse whisper as if the words

hurt her throat. "Dropped her. That's when he must have dropped her."

Margaret asked, "He didn't take her out of the crib to change her nappy, did he?" It seemed to me that Margaret was saying *nappy* a lot.

"Sometimes he did, actually. And on that day, the poor little thing was teething, and she had caught a bit of a cold to boot. She had already had two rather messy nappies that morning, so I guess Branwell took her into the bathroom to sponge her off, and that's when he dropped her. Surely you know how awkward he is."

Margaret said, "So, actually, you never saw him drop her." It seemed to me that Margaret was saying *actually* a lot.

"I didn't even know he was home. I was in my room on the other side of the Jack-and-Jill."

"And when he dropped her, the baby didn't cry?"

"Of course not. She had gone unconscious."

"Was Nikki out of the crib when Branwell called to you?"

"Yes. He was shaking her, trying to get her to wake up."

"How do you know he dropped her in the bath-room?"

"They found traces of Nikki's blood on the bathroom floor, actually. How else would it have got there?"

"And you didn't notice the blood when you ran through the Jack-and-Jill after he called you."

"Of course not. The adrenaline was pumping, and I wanted to get to the nursery."

"What did he say when he called?"

"He called, 'Vivi, come here. Nikki's breathing funny.' I came running. Brannie was shaking her to wake her up."

"Was that the last he spoke? When he called to you that the baby was breathing funny?"

"Not quite. I came into the room and was shocked to see him shaking her. You should never, never shake a baby. It's quite dangerous, actually. Their little brains go sloshing around in their skulls and get nicked and battered. I screamed, *'Stop!'* and I grabbed the baby from him."

"Then what happened?"

"The poor little thing threw up. When I had her in my arms, she felt feverish. I was worried that she would choke on her vomit, so I cleared the vomit from her mouth with my fingers, and I sent Branwell into the bathroom to get a washcloth. 'Get a washcloth,' I yelled. I did a good bit of yelling, actually. He came back with a damp washcloth. That is probably when he tried to wipe the blood off the bathroom floor. I cleaned her up a bit, but as I held her . . . her breathing was . . . so . . . so hard." Vivian began to tear up. "This was not an ordinary little ear or nose thing. I screamed at him, 'What have you done?' And he just stared at me. He looked toward the Jack-and-Jill and said, 'I . . . I . . . I.' But Branwell just kept staring and making his mouth go and the only sound that came out was, 'I . . . I . . . I.' I yelled at him to call 911, and I started to do CPR. Branwell dialed. But when the operator came on, he wouldn't tell her what was wrong. I had to stop the CPR to take the phone from him."

Vivian folded her arms across her blue sweater and hugged her upper arms. She shuddered. "It sends shivers down my spine every time I think of what poor little Nikki is going through."

"Yes," Margaret said, "it is chilling."

Vivian said, "I want to thank you, Margaret. This rehearsal has been most helpful."

Margaret said, "I'm sure you will do very well."

"Yes, our little talk has helped me remember the details." Vivian took another cigarette from her purse, held it to her lips, and looked at me and nodded. I popped out of my seat, picked up the matches from the coffee table, and was able to strike one on the first try.

She held my wrist in the same place.

She thanked me again and then said, "Some people say 'God is in the details.' Others say it's the Devil."

Margaret replied, "Maybe it depends on who's reporting the details." She checked her watch and announced that supper was ready.

She took the chicken casserole from the oven, placed it on the table, and reached into the drawer for a serving spoon and told us to help ourselves.

At dinner we talked about Vivian's plans. She said that as soon as she finished giving her deposition she would be returning to England. "In a way, I am living on standby. If Nikki dies, I'll have to return to the States for the trial."

"Well, let's hope that won't happen."

"Of course, we all pray that won't happen. The Zamborskas were pleasant enough, and I enjoyed being here, but this whole assignment has certainly mucked up my plans." Brits must say *mucked up* instead of *messed up*.

"What plans are those?" Margaret asked.

"All of them, actually. I am truly anxious to get on with my life."

Margaret said, "I think I've heard everyone from the Masssachusetts Nanny to the Long Island Lolita say that. What exactly does 'getting on with your life' mean?"

"In my case, it means going to university."

"And study what?"

"The law. I hope to become a barrister."

"That would be nice. I think you will look darling in a peruke."

"Do you really?"

"Yes, I do."

"I understand they're quite expensive."

"Let me make this promise, Vivian. If you become a barrister, I shall buy you your peruke."

I didn't know what a *peruke* was, and I didn't want to ask. If it was spelled anything like it sounded, I could look it up or ask Branwell. (That was about the gazillionth time I had to remind myself that he had gone silent. But maybe peruke would be the icebreaker that would get him to talk.)

Vivian had another cigarette with her coffee. I volunteered to light it for her. She held my wrist again. Same wrist. Same place. And then before I pulled my wrist away, she smiled shyly and lip-synced, "Thank you, Connor."

Thursday has always been my lucky day.

*　　*　　*

Margaret dropped Vivian back at the hotel before she drove me home.

I asked her, "Why did you tell Vivian that you had changed your silverware drawers around? It's been in the same place ever since you've lived here."

"I lied."

"Why?"

Margaret shrugged. "I felt like it."

"Is that all you're going to say?"

"For the time being."

"What is a peruke?" I asked.

"One of those white wigs that British barristers plop on top of their heads when they are trying a case."

"Is that named after Mr. Peruke who invented it?"

"I don't think so."

"Why did you promise Vivian that you would buy her one?"

"I stand about as much chance of having to keep that promise as you have of waking up tomorrow speaking Farsi."

"Why don't you like her?"

"I don't have to. You like her enough for both of us."

"Why did you invite her over for dinner if you don't like her."

"I felt like it."

109

"Well, I think she's nice."

"I noticed."

The first time I saw Branwell at the Behavioral Center, I had said to myself that even before I knew all the details, I believed in him. And I still did. But after having had supper with Vivian, and having learned more of the details, I had some new thoughts about Branwell, and I wondered if the Branwell I thought I knew was the Branwell I knew.

My mind was as mixed-up as that sentence.

I also had some new thoughts about Vivian. And about Branwell with Vivian.

And when I awakened the next morning my thoughts were not about Branwell and Vivian but about Vivian and me. Vivian with me. She had invaded my dreams that night, and those dreams were different from any of the other dreams I had ever dreamed up until I lit that first cigarette and felt Vivian's hand holding my wrist. And she held my wrist in the same place each time and thanked me.

10.

Margaret came to school and brought me a copy of the 911 tape.

I called her Wonder Woman not because she had managed to get the tape in less time than it would take an ordinary human being but because she had managed to enter the cleverly guarded halls of Knightsbridge Middle School without a diplomatic passport or bulletproof vest. "Do you have any other miracles to share with me?"

"This," she said, reaching into her shoulder bag and bringing forth a tape player. "A miracle of miniaturization and efficiency."

I always liked to start my visits with Branwell by telling him the good news—when there was good news—so I asked her how Nikki was, and she told me that they were still weaning her off the respirator.

When I entered the Behavioral Center, the guard at the reception desk who kept the sign-in book and who inspected my backpack held up the packet of flash cards and asked if I was making any progress with them. I told her that it was too soon to tell. She examined the tape and player and asked, "Trying something new?"

"Anything to help."

When everything was back inside my backpack, she handed it over across her desk. "Good luck," she said, smiling.

I didn't exactly know what still weaning someone off a respirator meant. I guessed that that news was in the category of medium-good. Not as good as having Nikki breathing on her own or *tracking,* which would mean that she was interacting with her environment and was what everyone was waiting for. Not as bad as not being weaned. I should have asked Margaret for more details, but I wasn't that interested. I had other things on my mind.

So once Branwell was brought out and seated across

the table from me, I got the Nikki-news over with as quickly as possible. I wanted to get to the real stuff. Stuff that had been on my mind since last night.

I wanted to talk to him about Vivian. I wanted to talk to him about her so badly that I was glad the conversation would be one way. To be perfectly honest— I've really tried to be—I wanted Bran to know that I had spent practically a whole night with this person that he had been keeping from me.

I didn't tell him about the rehearsal for the deposition. I didn't even mention the deposition. I wasn't even thinking about the details she had rehearsed with Margaret. I was thinking about the blue jumper and the hair grip. And that's what I told him about. *Jumpers* and *hair grips*. He had to understand that I, too, knew her language.

I don't know how much of my fascination with her crept into what I was saying, but I guess a lot of it did. I didn't care. He had to understand that he, Branwell, was not the only one that she paid attention to.

Bran had always been a good listener, but now he sat slouched in his chair and stared at his hands in his lap. When I mentioned that Vivian had let me light her cigarettes, he finally looked up at me and shook his head slowly, slightly, sadly. As if I was to be pitied.

I was not to be pitied. I had lit her cigarettes. And she had held my wrist and said thank you each time, and one time she had not even bothered saying it out loud but had just lip-synced.

Maybe it was the look he gave me, or maybe it was because I had been thinking about it a lot—a whole lot—or maybe if I try to be as perfectly-perfectly honest with myself as I have tried to be about everything else, I would have to admit that I took the "conversation" to the next level because it was the one that had invaded my dreams.

"How about walking in on her in the bathtub?" I said.

Branwell stopped looking sad the minute I mentioned bathtub. Instead he blushed. (Branwell blushes easily.)

Then I said, "How about walking in on her in the bathtub the second time?" Branwell lowered his head so fast and so far, I thought it would separate from his neck. And he was blushing so much, I thought I could feel the heat of it across the table.

I should have stopped then and there, but I couldn't. I had to go on, and I said, "And the third time?" But now Branwell jerked his head up as hard as he had jerked it down. "Way to go, man," I said, trying to tease. And maybe if my mouth had not been so dry, that would have come out the way it should have. But it didn't. Branwell's jaw dropped, and he glared at me. He opened his mouth as if to speak, but nothing came. He sucked in his breath and tried again, and then he bolted up, overturning his chair, turned his back to me, and started to walk out.

"Bran!" I called. "Bran. Our time isn't up. Don't leave. Please," I said. "Please don't leave." He stood still, his back to me. "I brought a copy of the tape with me," I said. He turned his head and looked at me out of the corner of his eye. He looked like a frightened puppy. And I was frightened, too. What had I triggered? "The 911 tape," I said. He turned about three quarters of the way around, and I hurriedly took it from my backpack and put it on the table. "Here it is."

The guard came over and set his chair upright.

"Let's listen to the tape, Bran." He was facing me now, and so was the guard. "Please sit down. Let's listen to it together."

Bran sat down, and, nervous as I was, I managed to start the tape. As soon as the first words came on, he cocked his head and held his hand behind his ear to gather in the sound. Then when the tape got to the part where the operator said that she was transferring the call to Fire and Rescue—the same part where he had reacted when Big Beacham had played it—he leaned his head down on the desk, the way we had been taught Native Americans kept their ears to the ground to hear a buffalo herd.

When the tape finished playing, he sat up and made a whirling motion with his finger. He wanted me to play it again. And I did. This time he kept his ear low the whole time it played, and at that same point in the tape, he pounded with his fist—only once and not real hard—on the table. I knew there was something there that needed to be heard. I rewound the tape and asked him if he wanted me to play it again. He shook his head no.

I took the pack of flash cards from my pocket and put it on the table. The one marked TAPE was on top, faceup. Branwell's eyes fell on that card immediately, and he blinked twice very rapidly. Still nervous, still upset by his reaction to my mentioning the bathroom invasions, I asked, "The tape?" He blinked twice. "You want me to investigate the tape?" He blinked twice again, very rapidly. You could say he blinked in anger. "Good," I said, but didn't mean it.

Trying to put the best face I could on a very bad session, I said, "The tape it will be. I'll check on the tape." I tumbled everything—cards, cassette, cassette player—back into my backpack and waved good-bye. Which Bran didn't see, since he was already heading back to his quarters.

I left the Behavioral Center with the tape and with a very bad feeling. I should have found out if it was God or the Devil who was in the details of Vivian's deposition. But I had blown it. I couldn't go back to that topic. Not yet. Maybe never.

I had to do something with the tape. I knew that there were ways to improve the sound by bringing up the volume on the good parts and cutting out the static in other parts. I suspected that it was done on a computer, and if it was, Margaret would either know how to do it or where to get it done.

As I was leaving, the guard at the front desk asked me if I had made any progress. If you consider that I had gotten a violent response out of Branwell, you could say yes. But if you consider that he was still not speaking, and I still didn't know why, you would have to say no.

"Too soon to tell," I replied. I was becoming an expert at saying nothing by saying something: excellent training for politicians or talk-show hosts.

As soon as I got home, I called Margaret and told her about the tape. She explained that there is a way to enhance a tape, but it has to be sent away to a lab to do it. Then she thought a minute more. "There's a sound studio in the music department at the university. Maybe they have the equipment to do it. I'll call you back."

Margaret called me back to tell me that there was good news and bad news. The good news was that the school did have the equipment. The bad news was that the head of the sound lab said that he couldn't get to it until after Christmas. There was a long pause on the phone before she added, "You could ask your father if he could use his influence."

"He's your father, too."

"Remind him when you ask," she said, and hung up.

I guess Margaret and I will always disagree about our father. When I told him what I needed and why I needed it, he was not only willing to help, he was eager to. When I gave him the tape, he asked if it was a first generation copy—meaning if this was a copy from the original tape or a copy of a copy. I didn't know. I told him to call Margaret to find out.

I heard only his end of the call. He did not sound

like a father calling his daughter. He sounded like his other self—the university registrar calling for information. I imagined Margaret's end of the conversation, and I could guess that she sounded like a telemarketer giving details of the carpet-cleaning special of the week.

The good news was that it was first generation and good enough for the music department to digitize (or whatever they had to do). I only heard Dad's end of the conversation when he called the head of the student sound studio. He said, "I understand," three times. And then he said that he wouldn't be asking if these were ordinary circumstances. He said, "I understand," twice more. He also said that he would be willing to take the tape to a commercial lab, but he knew that the work done at the university was much better. And then he said, "I'll drop it by first thing in the morning." One more "I understand," and then, "I'll pick it up Monday afternoon."

I thanked him and told him that I would tell Margaret how helpful he had been. "That won't be necessary," he said.

11.

It was the first Saturday in December, the day that Margaret asked me to go to the mall with her so that we could buy Christmas presents for the family. I had never had this kind of date with her before. Margaret is half-Jewish and doesn't do much about Christmas, but Hanukkah was only a week away, and she liked to give out her presents then.

Margaret didn't see clients on Saturday, but usually spent a half day in the office catching up on the paperwork. She had started out as a one-woman business, but now she has three others working for her. She favors hiring women. Most of her clients are doctors and dentists. She develops software that helps them manage patient care and accounting. Last year she developed a system for the Clarion County Hospital. That was the hospital where I was born and where I had had my tonsils removed when I was in fourth grade and where Nikki was now.

I decided to walk from my house to hers. I could have taken the city bus, which circles the campus, but it was a clear, crisp day, not too cold, and since I had been going to the Behavioral Center after school, I had not spent much time out-of-doors.

Halfway across campus, I was over The Ditch and, out of habit, I stopped on the bridge and began looking for lovers. I spotted a couple in bright quilted jackets with their arms around each other's waists weaving their way down to the bottom of the gorge. When Branwell and I were little, we would run to another place on the bridge and try to find them again. If we did, we would yell, "Spot."

They wound in and out of view, then around a bend and out of sight. I didn't move.

Since the night before last, for the first time in all the years I had been going to the gorge, I was not interested in watching. For the first time in all these years, I wondered how it would feel to be part of a couple. How it would feel to have someone other than Branwell to take a walk with.

The lovers came into view again. They still had their arms around each other. They could hardly feel as much of each other as I had felt when Vivian had touched my bare wrist. Without trying too hard, if I closed my eyes and concentrated, I could still feel her fingers on my wrist (she had held the same one in the same place each time) and see her face as she thanked me for lighting her cigarette.

I remembered that day in September, the last time Bran and I had met over The Ditch, that day he had said, "She calls a motorcycle a *motorbike* and a truck, a *lorry*," and then had looked at me with that loony smile, and I had gotten sarcastic. Here was my lifelong friend changing before my very eyes. Here he was interested in taking a walk with someone other than me, someone who was female, an older woman, someone who had shown a lot of interest in him.

I have to admit that I had been jealous.

Yesterday had been payback time. I had wanted to make him jealous of me, and my secret feelings must have crept into my voice, just as his had crept into that loony smile.

How he must have hated hearing me talk about her blue jumper and her flaxen hair. So he had turned over his chair to shut me up just as my sarcasm had shut him up.

I guess the only way to keep secret thoughts secret is not to say anything. Even to your lifelong best friend. If you don't speak at all, you don't have to worry about saying the wrong thing or having the right thing interpreted wrong. And that is what Bran had done. He had stopped talking about Vivian. She became the unspoken.

I wondered if my sarcasm is what started it all. Maybe my sarcasm led to his silence about Vivian, and that led to more things *unspoken,* and the unspoken just deepened and darkened from that day in September to Columbus Day until the great wall of silence that was now.

Maybe.

But I don't think so.

Following that 911 call, his silence was not just a different size of the unspoken. It was a whole different species. Before, he could talk but would not. Now he would if he could, but he can't. Something had caused a serious disconnect.

After learning the details of Vivian's deposition, I had begun to have doubts about my friend. How much of that had crept into my voice yesterday when I began asking him about the Jack-and-Jill bathroom? Was that what had angered him?

Vivian had once again come between us.

I looked down into the empty gorge and was suddenly terrified. Being Branwell's only bridge to the outside world, I was in a position of power. I realized that I could destroy my friend.

If I had let Bran walk out when he had turned over the chair, I would have broken the last connection between him and me. If I was to continue as Branwell's friend and as his bridge to the outside world, I had to believe in him as I had the day of my first visit to the Behavioral Center before I learned the first detail. I was now the one who had to leave my thoughts and dreams of Vivian unspoken and let the information take me where it would.

SIAS: Silence does for thinking what a suspension bridge does for space—it makes connections.

I gave myself four stars.

I found Margaret in her office, staring at her computer screen.

"No news. They're still weaning Nikki off the respirator."

It had not occurred to me until that minute that Margaret was keeping tabs on Nikki through her computer. I should have known that Dr. Zamborska would hardly be calling her with reports. I don't know if what she was doing could properly be called *hacking,* but I didn't care if it was.

"Dad got the guy at the sound lab to enhance the tape."

"So he did," Margaret said, not taking her eyes off the computer screen.

"He was very helpful."

"Yes, The Registrar has a way with underlings."

I usually didn't answer Margaret's sarcasm about Dad. But because of what I had been thinking about Branwell and how my sarcasm had led to the unspoken, this time I did. "Margaret," I said, "I think you're awful hard on Dad. He didn't even want me to tell you that he had been helpful."

"So are you telling me to grow up?"

"Maybe I am."

She turned away from the computer and, looking straight at me, said the strangest thing. "Connor, suppose for this Christmas I give you something very beautiful—say, a beautiful ivory carving."

"I wouldn't mind," I said.

"This gift has been made with care and given to you to keep forever. It is intricately and deeply carved. There are no rough edges. All of it is polished, and all of it is pure ivory."

"What would be wrong with that?"

"Nothing would be wrong with it if it came with instructions and a warning."

"What instructions?"

"That it must be oiled now and then or it will get brittle, and pieces will break off."

"And what's the warning?"

"That ivory comes from a living organism, so it is bound to change as it ages. Ivory darkens. A day comes when you have to put this beautiful thing away. So not knowing about maintenance and aging, you put it in a drawer and close the drawer. Time goes by, and the gift giver wants to see his gift. So you take it out of the drawer, and both of you are surprised that it isn't what it was. It doesn't look the same. Without maintenance, delicate pieces have broken off, and some of the places where the carving was very deep have darkened to the color of a tobacco stain. You haven't been careless; you have just never been warned about the changes that happen with time, and you haven't been taught proper maintenance. But you know one thing—you are never going to put this gift on display again."

Margaret and I looked at each other. "You're talking about love, aren't you?"

"I knew I didn't have a dummy for a brother."

"Are you basing all this on the way you felt about Dad and the divorce?"

"What else would I have to base it on, Connor?"

"But, Margaret, it wasn't Dad's fault if his gift changed with time. You said yourself when something comes from a living organism, it is bound to change as it ages. Well, love comes from *two* living organisms. You should expect twice as many changes."

Margaret stared at her computer screen. "I wasn't warned." She waited a long time before she added, "If I am very honest with myself—and on occasion I can be, you know—when Dad fell in love with your mother, I felt left out."

I wondered if I had been so irritated with Branwell that day on the bridge because I had felt left out. Before I could decide, I heard Margaret say, "I was definitely left out of that relationship."

"You wanted to be included in their love affair?"

"In the romance of it. Listen, Connor, I was just about your age when it all happened, so what should I know about romance?"

"I thought you just said that you didn't have a dummy for a brother."

"I don't. That's why I know you understand."

"Am I to understand that you're also talking about Branwell?"

"I am. I can relate to him because a lot of what happened to him happened to me. I often think about Branwell last summer. Here he was just returned from a month with The Ancestors, who had long ago laid down the rules. Rules they are very definite about. All that was required to keep their love was total obedience. Being in need, Branwell obeyed. He did all that they required. He wore a jacket for dinner every night and took golf and tennis lessons he didn't want or need. He was the perfect grandson, reflecting their perfect love. Then he comes home, ready to be Dr. Z's perfect son. And what does he find? He finds that Dr. Z has allowed someone to whittle the ivory. The rules for keeping everything perfect had changed." Margaret pursed her lips to keep the words inside until they were fully formed, and then she said, "I think Branwell felt cheated."

"Cheated of what?"

"Of their happiness. Seeing other people's happiness always makes us feel cheated."

I think I felt cheated that day on the bridge when I saw how happy Bran was about Vivian. I asked, "Do you think Branwell fell in love with Vivian . . . that way? The way that Dr. Zamborska loves Tina?"

Margaret did not answer immediately. Then she said, "Yes, Connor, now that you mention it, I think he did."

"You mean . . . you mean . . . like sex?"

Margaret laughed. "I think the s-word was part of it. I think Vivian enriched his fantasies." Margaret tilted her head so that her face was level with mine. She read what I was thinking. "Vivian seems to be something of a specialist at that."

My thoughts of love for the past two days were more like Silly Putty than carved ivory. I wanted to say something that would lead Margaret offtrack, but when I opened my mouth to make some smart remark, nothing came out. I remembered my resolution on the bridge and decided that this was as good a time as any to start leaving my thoughts of Vivian unspoken.

Margaret put her arm across my shoulder. "It's all right, Connor. When I was your age, I had a mad crush on my social studies teacher."

I didn't like her calling what I was feeling *a mad crush*. It sounded so juvenile.

When Margaret and I split up at the mall so that we could buy presents for each other, I knew that that would be my chance to get to a shop that sold hair grips. What I got was not exactly a barrette. It was more of a hair ornament. It was shaped like a butter-fly, but it had tiny claws to *grip* the hair. It was a milky blue (the clerk called it opalescent) and had a few rhinestones (the clerk said they were in good taste) along the edge. I could hardly wait to give it to her.

When we did hook back up at the mall, Margaret did not (thank goodness) ask me what I had in any of my bags. She did ask me what I had gotten Dad.

"A Hawaiian shirt for dress-down Fridays."

"Perfect choice," she replied, "as long as it has long sleeves, a starched collar, and is worn with a necktie."

"What did you get him?"

"A priority listing on a heart transplant."

With a sister like Margaret, there is no such thing as a perfect reply, a perfect conversation, or a perfect carving in ivory.

DAYS TWELVE & THIRTEEN

12.

There was little to report when I visited Bran on Sunday.

First, I told him that my father was getting the tape digitized.

Second, I reported on my shopping trip with Margaret. (True to my resolution, I did not mention buying a gift for Vivian.) I told him who I had run into at the mall.

Most of the kids were surprised to see me out and around. They had noticed how I had been ducking all invitations to join them for ice skating at Fivemile Creek Park or for kicking a soccer ball around. It was clear to them that I was a guy on a mission, and they knew what it was.

Most of them had asked about him. Some acted like a bunch of rubberneckers at the scene of an accident and asked a lot of questions. *What has he done? What is wrong with him? Has he lost his mind?* I couldn't give them answers. Because I didn't know what he had done or what was wrong with him or whether he had lost his mind. There were a lot of rumors about him. Almost all of them were not true, but to deny the untrue ones would let everyone know that I had inside information. Not enjoying Branwell's advantage of being struck dumb, the kids expected me to speak. So I did the next best thing. I played only one note. Whether it was a rumor or a question, I gave everyone the same answer: "You'll have to talk to Gretchen Silver. She's in the yellow pages under *mouthpieces.*"

Some of the kids asked about him because they care. Kids who are not frightened by differences admire Branwell for his. Because way down deep they know that civilized people have to preserve rare birds.

Third, I talked about school, what he and I call day care. I complained a lot. I enjoy complaining. There are only three weeks of school between Thanksgiving and Christmas, and each one of them is a pain in the neck. By the time you wind down from Thanksgiving, you have to rev up for Christmas, and between the celebrations and special holiday projects, the teachers feel they have to squeeze in the regular amount of curriculum so that we can get decent scores on the achievement tests. They keep telling us that if we don't look good, they don't look good. They sound like a shampoo commercial.

In-depth complaining is fun only when you have a sympathetic listener. Even though listening was about the best thing that Branwell had been doing lately, he hardly looked at me the whole time I talked. I found it exhausting. It is not easy carrying on both halves of a conversation and having to avoid words that are on the top of your mind. Words like *jumper* and *hair grip* and certain proper nouns like *Vivian*.

On Monday, our class used up practically our whole lunch hour practicing for our Holiday Concert. Branwell had been given a solo part in our arrangement of the John Lennon song "Imagine." (Branwell did love the Beatles.) "We missed you at chorus rehearsal today," I said. "They decided to eliminate the solo. I'm telling you, Bran, we do a lot better when you're there." Branwell hardly looked up at me. I waited for some reaction—anything—but he stared at his hands, which were in his lap. I got up to leave, and he stared at the chair where I had been sitting. It didn't seem to matter whether I was in it or not.

I left without bringing out the flash cards.

I took the city bus home, and the minute I walked into the kitchen, I saw the tape on the table. Dad had put it there—no note or anything. My father is not the kind of person who would write a note. He would expect me to know what it was and why it was there. That was his way of letting me know that—even though he was almost never there when I came home from school—he knew that the kitchen was always my first stop.

I called Margaret.

I can always tell when she has a client in her office. She talks to me as if I am one. "Yes," she said when I told her the tape had arrived. "Yes, I'll be here at four-thirty." She paused. I did not say a word. Then she added, "Please bring it with you. We can check on it then." Another pause. "I look forward to seeing you at four-thirty." I sometimes think that I am the only male on the planet that she looks forward to seeing.

I grabbed a glass of OJ and snarfed down three Oreos without even sitting down. I had the tape in my pocket and was out the door within three minutes of hanging up and within a hundred feet of catching the city bus to Old Town.

Margaret was still in her office when I got to Schuyler Place. I jerked my head toward her computer. "How's Nikki doing?"

"They've taken her off the respirator. She's breathing on her own." Margaret smiled. She knew then that I knew that she was hacking into the hospital records. She also knew that by never saying anything, she would never have to admit or deny it.

"That's wonderful," I said. "I wish I had known before I went to see Branwell today."

"Nikki is technically out of a coma now, but she is not really responding yet. She's in a vegetative state."

"After today's session with Branwell, I'm not sure that Nikki is the only one in a *vegetative state*. How long will this last?"

"No one knows. And that makes it extra hard. It could last a week or a month or a year or forever."

"Don't say that, Margaret. It sounds scary."

"It is scary."

"What does Nikki have to do to get out of it?"

"Do purposeful things."

"Like what kind of purposeful things can an infant do?"

"She can follow an object with her eyes, for example. Or smile when she recognizes her mother."

"Every time I go to the Behavioral Center, I look over the list on the sign-in book, and I never see Tina's name. Do you think she's ever gone there to see Branwell?"

"I doubt it."

"Don't you think it would help Bran out of *his* vegetative state if she did?"

"Probably."

"Do you think Tina blames Branwell for what happened?"

"In a word, yes. I'm guessing now, but I think she believes that Branwell is stonewalling, that his silence is just a stubborn refusal to talk about what happened."

"Do you think that?"

"No, Connor, I don't. As a matter of fact, I'm convinced that Branwell was struck dumb because he has a terrible secret of which he dare not speak."

Margaret shut down her computer, and we moved into the living room to listen to the tape.

In the spot where Branwell brought his clenched fist to his mouth, the part where the operator says that she is transferring the call to Fire and Rescue—the place where Branwell had put his ear to the table—there was a man's voice. It was hard to make out what he was saying, but it sounded like, *What happened, what happened?* There was also Vivian saying, *Go! Go!* I asked Margaret if she knew who that man's voice belonged to. Sadly, she shook her head no. "It's obvious there was someone in the house besides Vivian and Branwell."

"I think we have a suspect," I said.

"Or a witness."

"Either way, there was someone there who can help us get the facts."

"If we can find out who that is."

"Do you want to come with me when I take him the tape?"

Margaret said that she did not think it was wise—yet. "It's you he trusts. I'll be there for him when the time is right. And I'll be here for you until then."

I hugged her.

"Enough mushy stuff," she said.

13.

The phone rang early. Dad answered because most early morning calls are for him. I heard him say, "It was no trouble, really. . . . I'm glad it worked out. . . . Please don't hesitate to ask if there's anything else I can do. . . . Yes, I'll tell him." It was Margaret. I knew it was. I was at Dad's side with my hand stretched out for the receiver before he even had a chance to call me to the phone.

"What's up?" I asked.

"I wanted to tell you that I think it's a good idea to mention to Branwell that Nikki is off the respirator but that it's not a good idea to use the term *vegetative state*."

I started to tell Margaret that I had lately had a lot of

practice in avoiding using certain words in certain conversations, when I realized that that was not why she had called. She had just wanted an excuse to call and thank Dad. "Thanks," I said, "thanks for reminding me." Then, cupping the mouthpiece, in something just above a whisper, I said, "Dad is pleased you called."

"How can you tell?"

"He smiled."

"Check him out after they remove the sutures."

"Margaret . . .," I interrupted before she got really rolling, "Margaret . . ."

"What?"

"Thanks for calling. I've got to get to school now. See you later."

The first thing I did was tell Branwell that Nikki was off the respirator. I think he already knew, because he didn't look surprised when I told him. Then I put the digitized tape on the table, and if I tell you that his smile was a real genuine grin from ear-to-ear, that still does not tell you what that smile meant to me. It was like a signpost. A signpost that I was on the right road.

Branwell and I listened to the tape together. When the sound of the man's voice came up, he tapped on the table. I rewound and played it again. He leaned back and squinted his eyes. He made a motion like someone was dealing a deck of cards. So I pulled my flash cards out of my pocket and laid them out on the table. The males I had cards for were Dr. Zamborska and Grandfather Zamborska and The Ancestor. His eyes skirted past all three of them.

He stared at me like a puppy that needs to be let out real bad. He needed me to let him out. I had to find a way. I was not real comfortable being in this position of power. I liked it better when Bran and I were equals.

And then I had a flash. I just had to refine our method of communication. I remembered that the paralyzed author of *The Diving Bell and the Butterfly* had his assistant recite the alphabet—rearranged according to how frequently the letters were used—and the author would blink his left eye when the letter he wanted came up. I wouldn't have to recite the alphabet for Branwell. I could write it.

This is what I did. I turned all of the flash cards over. There were twelve of them, remember. I wrote the letters of the alphabet on the backs—two to a card, except for the last two, which had three each. I had no chance to arrange the letters in any order except the way we had learned them in kindergarten—

alphabetically. Besides, except for the vowels, I hardly knew which were used the most—although, judging from the number of points you get for certain letters in Scrabble, it was an easy guess that X and Q don't come up too often.

I didn't have any extra paper with me except for a Snickers wrapper that I had put in my pocket because I didn't want to litter. It was one of those mini bars that we gave out at Halloween. I opened it up, and it made a neat little square, the inside was white, and even though it was waxy, I found I could write on it.

Using my pencil, I pointed to the letters one at a time and watched for Branwell to blink twice. It was awkward at first. I would look down at the letter to make sure my pencil was positioned all right, and then I would quickly look at Branwell so I wouldn't miss the blink of his eye. But by the time I got to the middle of the alphabet, I had gotten smoother, and we—both of us—were concentrating so hard, I think we generated enough current to connect our brain waves.

The first letter was M. I started back at A and pointed very pointedly at the vowels because I knew a vowel would follow. It was O. Then came R. And Branwell blinked four times. He meant for me to double the R, but I didn't take the hint, so I started back at A and pointed to them, one at a time, until we again got to R. The letter I followed the double R, and by then, I guessed that S would end it all, and it did. I had MORRIS on the little Snickers wrapper. I showed it to Branwell, and he blinked twice. Morris was no one I knew.

I started the process again so that I could find out what the second name was. I got to J, and Branwell blinked four times. I wrote JJ on the paper. I wanted a vowel between those two J's, but Branwell blinked twice, telling me that JJ was right. I started at the top of the alphabet again, and he stopped me at the letter S. So I had MORRIS JJS, and I was not happy. I even said, "Morris. J. J. S.," out loud, and Branwell nodded that I was right. He even managed a weak smile at my confusion.

I started folding up the little square of Snickers paper to put it back in my pocket, and Branwell reached across the table and put his fingertips on the back of my hand. It was the first that he had touched me since he had been sent to the Center, and it was so unexpected that I involuntarily pulled my hand back. Then, worried that I had hurt his feelings, I reached over the table to pat his hand, and he pulled his hand back and dropped both of his hands into his lap. His nostrils were flared, and he looked frightened. I said, "Cool it, Bran." And then realization hit me. He didn't want me to put the Snickers square away. He wanted me to go through the alphabet again. It was like playing a crazy game of charades—except that I had to play both sides—the acting out and the guessing. "New word?" I asked.

Branwell nodded yes.

I started again marking off the letters one at a time. He stopped me at P, then I, then he blinked four times at Z, and I knew that the final letter would be A. But, what the heck, A was at the top of my list, so I pointed to it and let him blink.

MORRIS JJS PIZZA. Of course. I said, "Morris works at JJ's Pizza? Is that it?" I asked, tapping the tape with one hand and the Snickers square with the other.

He blinked twice.

"I'll do my best," I said.

I folded the little square of paper again and put it in my pocket. This time Branwell made no effort to stop me. I stacked my deck of cards, put a rubber band around them, dropped them in my backpack, and said, "Way to go, man," and wished I hadn't. But if Branwell made a connection between my saying it now and my saying it about the Jack-and-Jill, he didn't show it. He didn't turn over any chairs. He smiled.

I left the Behavioral Center feeling that Branwell's smile had been a signpost on the road to *re*covery. Nikki was on it, and so was Branwell. And I was on the road to *dis*covery. And that had a nice ring to it. Or it would have, if I had said it out loud.

I went directly to Margaret's. Her office hours were over, so I walked around back and knocked on her door. Margaret came running out of the kitchen, swung open the door and said, "Well?"

"It's Morris who works at JJ's Pizza."

"It's a grand night for pizza," she said. "You better call your mother and The Registrar and tell them you won't be home for supper."

"Just what I was thinking," I replied.

JJ's has been in business forever. It's down by the railroad tracks. The restaurant itself is in the old station house. It's not part of a chain, it's not in a good section of town, and it makes the best pizza anyone has ever put in his mouth. When I was little, JJ's never delivered. Now they do, but a lot of their business still comes from people who go there to hang out and buy a slice or a pie.

The sit-down part of JJ's was not very busy. There was only one server, but there were two women working behind the counter where people fill orders for takeout. Margaret and I took a booth and waited. When the server came over, she put two napkins on the table and asked, "What can I get you to drink?" Margaret told her two Cokes, one Diet, and before she could turn away—they're always in a hurry after they take your drink orders—Margaret asked if Morris was around.

"Which Morris?" she asked.

"What's my choice?"

"There's Morris in the kitchen—we call him Moe—and there's Morris who delivers."

Margaret took a guess. "Morris who delivers."

"He's out on a delivery." She swept her hand around the almost-empty room. "Don't let this fool you. We are busy, but it's all takeout. I've taken more calls than the cell phone tower on Greene Street. We always get busy with deliveries the week before final exams. Everyone gains weight during exam week."

"When will Morris be back?"

"Can't tell. But you'll know when he is. He has to come up here to pick up new orders." She flipped through a pile of forms. "He's got these to do."

Margaret said, "Maybe we'll be lucky, and he'll show up while we're here."

"Eat slow," I said.

Margaret replied, "Good idea."

I was an inch away from the back crust on my second slice and was pulling air through the straw of my Coke when a guy wearing a black leather jacket with metal studs on the collar and the pockets came in. He also had a stud in his nose and two rings—small metal ones pinching his right eyebrow. Both ears had diamond studs, but the left one also had a silver skull that hung almost to his shoulder. His right wrist was tattooed with a circlet of what looked like fish scales (but they could have been dragon scales). His head was shaved except for a tuft that ran the distance from his forehead to his neck. It was all one length, but two colors. The roots were black, and the top third was bright yellow.

Margaret went over to the counter. "Are you Morris?" she asked.

He looked up from the pile of orders only long enough to answer, "Since I been born," before going back to flipping through the orders, rocking as if he were listening to some secret music in his head.

"Hey, Darlene," he called, "how many of these are filled?" he asked, holding up the pile of papers.

"All except the one to Hobart Hall. Pepperoni and mushrooms. Large."

"Hobart Hall? Large goes without saying."

Darlene replied, "I think that lady wants to ask you something."

Morris looked up. "Yeah? Whatcha wanna know?"

By this time, I, too, was standing by the counter. I asked, "Do you know Branwell Zamborska?"

"Branwell Zamborska? What is that? Some kinda flavoring?"

"Branwell. Zamborska. He's my friend. Do you know him?"

"Does he have an order in for pizza?"

"No, no," I said. "He's my friend. He's over at the Behavioral Center."

"We don't deliver there. Not allowed."

"That's not what I'm asking," I said.

"What, then?"

"My friend, Branwell. He's in trouble. He can't speak."

"Listen," Morris said, "I can tell you, this Branwell wouldn't be over at the Behavioral Center if he weren't in trouble. Ain't that the truth, Darlene?"

"He knows you," I said.

"How do you know that?"

"He told me."

"I thought you said he couldn't speak. Did I hear that from you, or didn't I? Didn't you just tell me that he couldn't speak? So, tell me, how could he tell you that he knows me?"

"We have a way. We have a way of communicating."

"What's that?"

"A way."

"Well, whatever is your way, kid, it's inaccurate. I don't know no Branwell Zamborska." He glanced down at the stack of orders. "I gotta get outta here." He looked over at the counter at Margaret and then at me. He opened his mouth as if he were about to say something, then closed it and looked aside. "Sorry, kid," he said. And then he left.

Margaret and I went back to our booth, but the only thing I could swallow was the lump in my throat. Margaret noticed and asked if I was finished. I could hardly speak, so I nodded yes, and she said, "Let's get out of here."

We were no sooner in the car than she said, "He's lying."

That cheered me up.

"How do you know?"

"The name, Branwell Zamborska, rolled off his tongue a little too easily. He was familiar with it. He's heard it before."

"Why do you think he lied?"

"People lie for only one reason, Connor. Fear."

"You lied to Vivian because you felt like it. That's what you told me."

"Can't you ever forget anything I tell you?"

"I'd be lying if I told you I could."

She laughed. "Well I think Morris JJ's Pizza is lying out of fear. Fear of knowing too much. He's protecting someone. And someone may be himself. Or he could be protecting something."

"What something could he be protecting?"

"Well, I'm pretty sure the something he's protecting is not secret information about our space program. He hardly looks like a rocket scientist."

"But he's not dumb." I thought about the way he had looked at me and said, "Sorry, kid." There was something soft in his voice. "I don't think he's as tough as he is trying to look either."

"I agree with that, little brother. We have to find out his last name. Maybe he's a student at the university. Maybe The Registrar can help us find out."

"I doubt if he's a student. I don't think students spend their nights delivering pizzas the week before exams. Why don't we just go back and ask Darlene?"

Margaret laughed. "Maybe that was a little too obvious. I'll check it out tomorrow. It's pretty clear that Morris JJ's Pizza knows something, and I think we ought to investigate before we confront Branwell with it. Maybe you should skip your visit to Branwell tomorrow."

"He'll want to know what I found out about Morris JJ's Pizza."

"There won't be much to tell him."

"I know. But he may be able to give me another hint."

"A good lawyer never asks a witness a question she doesn't know the answer to."

"But, Margaret, I'm not trying to be a good lawyer. I'm trying to be a good friend."

14.

The phone rang as I was almost out the door to catch
the school bus. Dad had already left for the office, so
Mom answered. There is a certain tone in her voice—
polite but strained—that tells me that Margaret is on
the other end. So to spare my mother's having to make
conversation and to keep myself from missing the bus,
I took the receiver from her without being called.

"Hi. What's up?"

"I got a call late last night from Morris JJ's Pizza."

"How did he find you?"

"The sales slip. I charged the pizza. I'm in the phone
book."

"Did he say he remembered Branwell?"

"I think he was about to, but he hung up."

"Did he say anything?"

"He said, 'Is this Margaret Rose Kane,' and I said it was. Then he said, 'This is Morris from JJ's,' and I said, 'Oh, hello.'"

"Why did you waste time saying that? You already said hello once."

"How was I supposed to know he was about to hang up?"

"What else did he say?"

"He asked if that kid—meaning you—who was with me was my brother. I admitted you were. He asked if you go to Knightsbridge Middle, and I said you did. He asked when was school out, and I told him. Then he said, 'I was thinking about . . . ,' and I heard another voice, and that's when he hung up."

"Was it a male voice?"

"Not sure. It was muffled like he had his hand shielding the mouthpiece."

"Did it sound like his mother?"

"How should I know? I don't even know if he has a mother."

"Everyone has a mother, Margaret. Between us, we have two."

"It's far too early in the morning for you to be giving me biology lessons, Connor. I'm calling to tell you that I had my machine on when he called, so I'll save the tape. If you want to come over to my place after you see Branwell, we can listen to it together."

"Déjà vu all over again."

She hung up.

School was a bummer. I could not stop thinking about Morris JJ's Pizza, about the 911 tape, and Vivi, Vivi, Vivian.

On the 911 tape, Vivian says, *He dropped her. He* could be Morris JJ's Pizza who *dropped her*.

The late afternoon sky looked like someone had rolled aluminum foil from horizon to horizon. My mood matched. As I approached the Behavioral Center, I saw a figure leaning against the corner of the building near the entrance. At first I thought that it was someone Margaret had sent to tell me that something had come up at work and that we would have to listen to her phone tape some other time. Then when I was within a block of the building, I saw that it was Morris JJ's Pizza. He was slouched against the edge of the building, holding a lighted cigarette. I stood still as I watched him take a long drag, drop it, and rub it out with his black boot. "Hey, kid," he said.

I answered, "Hey."

He pushed off from the building and started walking toward me. "On your way to see someone?"

"Yeah, my friend."

"That Branwell kid?"

"Yeah."

"How's he doing?"

"It's hard to say. He still can't talk."

Morris JJ's Pizza was walking beside me now. He jerked his head toward the other side of the street. There was a city bus stop there. It had a bench and one of those plastic dome shelters. We crossed the street and sat down. "What's going to happen to your friend?" he asked.

"I don't know. Depends on what happens to Nikki. If she pulls out of this, he may just be tried for reckless endangerment. If she doesn't, well, then I guess he'll be accused of manslaughter."

"I was there." He said it without apology, without explanation. He simply said, "I was there." My first reaction was to say something sarcastic. *Had a brain transplant to improve your memory?* Maybe I was too startled to say something like that. Maybe I didn't really think of something that smart until later. And maybe I was learning that sometimes saying nothing is a very good choice.

"I didn't see what happened," he said. "I was in Vivi's room when I heard the kid yell."

"Do you remember what he yelled?"

Morris didn't answer immediately. He took a pack of cigarettes out of his jacket pocket and tapped the bottom so that one of them flipped up. He started to take it out but didn't. He tapped it back down and slipped the pack into his inside jacket pocket. "Yeah, I do," he said. "I remember. He yelled, 'Vivi, come here. It's Nikki.'"

"What did Vivian do?"

"She popped off the bed and ran through the bathroom—the one that connects the two bedrooms—and started yelling at Branwell. I heard her say, 'Here, take her,' just before she rushed back to her bedroom to put on the rest of her clothes." He glanced at me for only a second before his eyes skittered away.

"Were you . . . ?"

Looking down, addressing the sidewalk under our feet, he said, "Yeah, we were." He lifted his head and let out so deep a breath that a white plume stayed suspended from his mouth. I almost expected it to fill with words like one of those balloons on the comic pages.

"Was Nikki awake when you arrived?"

"No. We waited until it was time for Nikki to take her nap."

Morris JJ's Pizza looked across the street—not at me—and addressed the yellow bricks of the Behavioral Center. "Vivi and I got dressed about as fast as we ever have. Luckily we haven't had time to get altogether undressed. Vivi, she races back through the bathroom to the nursery. I follow. I see Branwell with the baby on the floor. He's giving her mouth-to-mouth. Vivi takes the baby from him and tells him to call 911. I see the kid dial. Then he looks up and sees me coming through the bathroom. I ask, 'What happened?' I repeat, 'What happened?' Vivi shoos me out of there. 'Go! Go!' she says. And I go." He reached for his cigarettes again. "Like I said, I didn't see what happened."

"Do you know how long it was between the time Branwell came in and the time he called for Vivi?"

He stabbed at the pack of cigarettes, took one out of the pack, and didn't answer until he lit it. "No," he said, extending his lower lip and blowing the smoke upward. "But like I told you, it wasn't time enough for us to get undressed. I didn't hear nothing until I heard him call."

"You did hear him yell, 'Vivi, come here. It's Nikki.'"

Holding the cigarette between his first two fingers, he pointed with it. "That's what I heard."

"So the baby was breathing funny when Branwell came home from school."

"Now, I didn't say that. 'Vivi, come here. It's Nikki' don't mean that. Like maybe the baby was breathing normal when the kid comes home from school, and the kid was the one who did it. He could've been the one to make her breathe funny. I didn't know he was even there. He could've pounded her head on the floor like the bathroom floor or he could've had her to hit her head against the bathtub, for all I seen." He was facing the yellow brick wall across the street, but then he looked at me out of the corner of his eye. When he saw me watching him, he focused on the yellow brick wall. "Vivi, she's real worried."

"Is she worried that Branwell will be able to speak and tell the agency that Nikki was breathing funny when he found her?"

"Nah. Vivi's not worried about anything Branwell might say."

"So what is she worried about?"

"Her career."

"What career?"

"As an au pair. She says that the agency won't place her if they find out."

"Find out what?"

He looked directly at me. "Someone might tell them that she's started in smoking again." He smiled and took a long drag on his cigarette. "She don't look it, but she's real high-strung, and with all that's happened, she's back to smoking to soothe her nerves."

"Morris?"

"What?"

"Are you in love with Vivi?"

"Dunno 'bout me. But I'm sure about him."

"Branwell?"

"Yeah, Branwell," he said. "Brannie thinks she hung the moon." He took another long drag on his cigarette and let it drop to the ground. He danced around it for a minute, studying it, then he stamped it out. "Gotta go," he said.

"Morris?"

"What?"

"Will you tell me your last name?"

"Sure. It's Ditmer. Morris Ditmer. Spelled the way it sounds."

He pulled his *motorbike* keys out of his pocket with one hand and waved good-bye with the other.

I crossed the street to the Behavioral Center, so lost in thought that I was startled when Margaret approached and said, "Penny for those thoughts."

"Oh! Hi, Margaret," I said. "I just had a conversation with Morris."

"What did he have to say?"

I took a long look at my sister. I realized that she had been waiting, watching us from across the street. She probably suspected that Morris wanted to meet me when he asked what time I got out of school, but she had not come over, had not interrupted at all. She just watched. Probably the whole time we had been there. She didn't trust Morris, but she trusted me. Trusted me enough to allow me to find things out on my own. I said, "Thanks," and she knew what it was for.

"Blue peter," she said.

"His name is Morris Ditmer. He was there on the day it happened. But he didn't see what happened. He didn't see Branwell drop the baby. Didn't even hear him come in. He was in Vivian's room and, as they say, otherwise engaged. He says that the first thing he heard was Branwell's yelling, 'Vivi, come here. It's Nikki.' But he emphasized that for all he knew, Branwell could have been the one that made it happen."

Suddenly Margaret asked, "Do you have your pack of cards with you?"

I reached into my backpack and pulled them out. Margaret hesitated, then asked me to tell her again what Branwell's reaction had been when I had teased him about Vivian. I told her how he had blushed at first but then he had gotten angry and had jumped up so fast that he overturned his chair and was ready to walk out on me. I had never before seen him look the way he had looked then.

"I think you should write *Jack-and-Jill bathroom* on one of those cards."

I figured that I would be telling Bran about my conversation with Morris and how Morris had admitted that Branwell had seen him in the bathroom that day. I found the card that had Margaret's name on it, crossed it out, and wrote BATHROOM.

"Good," Margaret said. "I don't think Branwell is ready to spell out exactly what happened, but——"

"Spell out? Are you making a pun?"

Margaret smiled. "Not intentionally."

After Margaret left, I went into the Behavioral Center, but I didn't sign in. The woman behind the desk knew me by now and called to me and said, "There's no one up there now, Connor. You can go up if you want to." I told her that I needed to straighten something out first. I sat down on one of those orange plastic chairs they have in the waiting area off to one side of the lobby. What I wanted to straighten out was my thoughts.

Something—something that lay as deep as my friendship with Branwell—was telling me that I should not have a card with the word BATHROOM written on it. Maybe I started thinking that because all of my other cards were things that Bran and I had between us. Maybe that is what started my thinking that BATHROOM didn't belong.

I sat there, trying to figure out what to do about the BATHROOM. I couldn't help but think about Branwell's reaction the day I had teased him about Vivian. I had never seen him act that way before. Something strong was driving him.

I sat there on the orange plastic chair and I thought and thought and thought. I don't even know if I could call what I was doing *thinking*.

This is what I know: In fourth grade, we learned about the Greek goddess Athena and how she was sprung—full-grown—from the forehead of Zeus. And that's the best way I can explain how the word *shame* sprang from me. I suddenly understood that shame was making Branwell silent. Something happened in that bathroom. Something that made Branwell ashamed.

The opposite of shame is respect, and Margaret had shown me a lot of respect. She always had. Like today, she had shown me a lot of respect by not interfering with my talk with Morris. When a person loses respect—self-respect or the respect of others—that's when he feels shame.

I had almost known that BATHROOM did not belong in my set of cards the moment Margaret had made the suggestion, but it wasn't until *shame* sprang full-grown from my head that I knew that I absolutely should not use it.

Maybe I wouldn't find out what happened that day of the 911 call unless Morris Ditmer told me, and maybe Morris Ditmer didn't really know. But that was a chance I had to take. Things change. Just yesterday, Morris Ditmer had said that he didn't even know Branwell Zamborska.

He knew something. And, sooner or later, he was going to tell. Otherwise, why would he have told me his last name?

Margaret had trusted me to handle Morris Ditmer without her. I knew she would understand why I decided not to show Branwell a card that said BATHROOM. I took the pack of cards from my backpack and, with a heavy black marker, I crossed it out.

I returned to the registration desk. As the woman examined the contents of my backpack, she said, "So you decided to go up anyway."

I smiled and nodded, glad I didn't have to explain.

Branwell had been waiting for me. I don't know how I knew. I just knew. So had the guard. I could tell that, too. I didn't take the cards out of my backpack at all, and that surprised them, too.

I told Branwell that I had seen Morris, that I knew his last name. I told him that Morris said to be sure to tell him that he didn't see what happened, but that he did hear him yell for Vivian and that he didn't know what time he had come in or what time Branwell had called. I left out the part about Morris's saying that for all he knew, Branwell could have been the one that made Nikki breathe funny. Then I said, "You'll never guess what he says Vivian is worried about." Branwell looked puzzled. "He says that she's worried that someone might tell the agency that she's started smoking again. I guess it's a rule that au pairs have to promise not to smoke."

Branwell looked agitated and started moving his hands in a pantomime of shuffling cards.

I got the cards out of my backpack. The one with the blacked-out BATHROOM was on top, so I slipped it off and let it fall into the backpack. I spread the cards out on the table. Branwell looked them all over and then made a flipping motion with his hand. I knew he wanted me to turn them over, so I did. He wanted the alphabet. He looked them over again, and, of course, the letters that were on the backside of the X'd-out MARGARET/blacked-out BATHROOM card were missing. I pulled the card out my backpack, allowing only the letter side—M and N—to show.

Now all the letters were laid out, and I started searching in my pockets for a piece of paper. Without saying a word, the guard put a notepad in front of me, and I thanked him by nodding and smiling in his direction. It was as if Branwell's silence had become contagious. I started pointing with my pencil. Branwell did not blink until I got to XYZ. He blinked twice at Y. Then O, then at L . . . and I needed no more letters to finish writing YOLANDA. Branwell blinked twice. I gathered up the cards. "I'll talk to her," I said.

Then Branwell opened his mouth as if to say something in reply, but nothing came out. I had the strange feeling that his silence had changed. It was strained. Whereas in the days past, Branwell had seemed to accept the fact that he could not speak, now he didn't. The change must have registered on my face, for

Branwell stood, quickly turned around, and nodded to the guard that he was ready to be returned to his room.

As I was taking the elevator down, I felt about as uneasy as I had felt going up, but for a different reason. Now I had a mission. I had to find Yolanda.

15.

Yolanda is the day worker who takes care of Mrs. Farkas who has multiple sclerosis and who lives across the street from the Zamborskas on Tower Hill Road. Yolanda works for Mr. and Mrs. Farkas every weekday afternoon from 1:30 to 5:30. In the mornings she helps some of the other families who live on our street. She cleans house for my mother on Friday mornings, and she goes to the Zamborskas' on Thursdays. After Nikki was born, Tina asked her to come on Monday mornings, too, to help with the laundry. Whether she was working for my mother or Tina, Yolanda always arrived on the 8:30 A.M. bus and worked until 12:30. Then she walked across the street, where she made lunch for Mrs. Farkas and herself. She helped Mrs. Farkas bathe, took care of the house, and prepared the evening meal before she left in time to catch the 5:35 city bus back downtown. She left the Farkas house at 5:30 and walked down to the bus stop, which is right across the street from my house at 184. That was her routine Mondays through Fridays.

I looked at my watch. It was five o'clock. I called my mother and told her that I'd be home late. She wanted to know how late, and I did a quick calculation. I could catch the city bus across the street from the Behavioral Center, at the stop where Morris and I had had our talk. I could ride the route all the way up to Tower Hill Road, where it would pick up Yolanda and then ride back down with her. If the bus left here at 5:15 and got to Yolanda's stop at 5:35, that meant twenty minutes up, twenty minutes back, and then twenty minutes to get back home again. "An hour," I told my mother.

It was my lucky day. Yolanda was standing by the curb waiting when the bus pulled up.

I caught the driver looking in his rearview mirror, waiting for me to get off. "This is the end of the line," he said.

"I know."

"Time to get off."

"I want to ride back down."

"Gotta pay another fare," he said.

"I don't have any more money with me," I said. "Can I charge it?"

"'Fraid not."

Yolanda had boarded and looked back and spotted me. "Why, Connor, what are you doing on the five thirty-five heading to town?"

"I really wanted to talk to you, Yolanda. Can you loan me the bus fare?"

Yolanda rode on a pass, but I couldn't, so she calmly reached into her pocketbook and took out her wallet and patiently counted out the exact change and dropped it in the slot. Then she slowly walked back and sat down next to me.

Yolanda is a person who can be more still than anyone. And she is equally good at doing one thing at a time. She is not like anyone who lives on Tower Hill Road and who are all university people except for Trevor James and John Hanson, who have Hanson-James House of Design. For example, if anyone else living on Tower Hill Road were waiting at the bus stop—not that any of them would, for they would either be driving or riding a bicycle, but, if they were—

they would be reading or brushing off their clothes or checking their watch. They would be doing something besides just waiting.

Waiting the way that Yolanda does it is an art. She's the same way when she's working. She picks something up and puts it back down before she goes on to the next thing. Sometimes she listens to music as she works, but that's not quite doing two things at once. I think Mrs. Farkas needs Yolanda's calming ways as much as she needs her helping hands.

Yolanda put her pocketbook on her lap and rested both her arms on top of it. "How is Nikki?" she asked.

"She's off the respirator."

"A good sign," she said, smiling. "And Branwell? Can he talk?"

"Not yet. But we have a way of communicating."

"That's nice. Friends always find a way to keep in touch."

"Branwell wanted me to talk to you, Yolanda. That's why I'm riding the bus back downtown. So that we can talk."

"What do you want to talk about?"

"About Vivian."

"You mean that English baby-sitter? I don't think Mrs. Zamborska should hire her back."

"Why not?"

"She smokes. Mrs. Zamborska did not allow anyone to smoke in the house and especially around the baby. Nobody allows that anymore. But that one smoked right there next to the nursery." She thought a minute and said, "That very first Monday I was there after she had come to live in, I caught her. I do the laundry on Monday. I had come upstairs to put the clean linens away. I stopped first at the nursery to put away the baby's things. The door to the bathroom was open, so I just walked in. What do I find but this Vivian taking a bath, lying there in water up to her neck. Her head was resting against the back of the tub, her face was pointing up. She was blowing smoke up toward the ceiling. I guess she didn't hear me come in because I obviously startled her. I said, 'Mrs. Zamborska doesn't allow smoking in the house.' She sat bolt upright and put her arms across her chest to cover up, still holding the cigarette. 'I didn't know,' she said. 'Doesn't that agency that placed you tell you that you shouldn't smoke around a baby?' She said that she wasn't told anything like that. I know that was a lie, but then she said that if Mrs. Zamborska didn't want her to smoke in the house, she wouldn't do it again. I asked her why she left the door to the baby's room open like that, and she said that she wanted to hear if the baby cried. I did wonder about that. After all, she had not heard me come clear into the bathroom."

"You do work really quiet, Yolanda. Maybe she couldn't hear you but could've heard the baby."

"Maybe. But she left the door open another time."

"When was that?"

"It must have been a Monday again. I know it was a laundry day. It was a school holiday. Let me think. It was sometime in October. What school holiday would you be having in October?"

"Columbus Day," I said, anxious now, thinking I was going to get some important background information. "Columbus Day is the only October holiday that was on a Monday."

"Then Columbus Day it must have been. I remember I arrived at eight-thirty. I always do. I picked up a laundry basket from the utility room—that room just off the kitchen, and I went into Branwell's room to change the bed linen and, much to my surprise, he was still in bed. I asked him if he was not feeling well, and that's when I found out it was a school holiday. He hopped out of bed and went into that little half-bath that is off the downstairs hallway. He still had to go upstairs for his showers, you know. He said that was all right because he always showered at night, and Vivian bathed in the morning. I told him to leave his pajamas on top of the washing machine. I do hate to have the odd piece hanging over, you know.

"I went upstairs. The baby was asleep. She's a pretty little thing, isn't she?"

"She sure is."

"When she opens those bright little eyes, it's like plugging in a string of Christmas lights, isn't it?"

"That's a beautiful way to put it, Yolanda."

"Well, that Monday, I went into the baby's room to gather up the laundry, and I saw that the door to the bathroom was open. I heard the water running. There was Vivian, sitting naked on the edge of the tub, running the water for her bath. I said to her, 'You better close that door.' Without looking up, she said, 'I told you, I can't hear the baby if I do.' I told her that it was a school holiday and that Branwell was home, and I didn't think she would want him walking in on her— naked as she was.

"'Oh!' she says. 'We can't satisfy a little boy's curiosity all at once, now, can we?' She winked at me in a way I didn't like. Didn't like at all. It was, I thought, sort of brazen. I also didn't like that *we. We* can't satisfy a little boy's curiosity. I never intended to. I am a very modest person. I just turned around and told her to keep the door closed and don't stay in the tub too long and bring her towels down to the laundry when she was through."

"Did Branwell hear any of this?"

"I can't imagine that he did. He was downstairs getting dressed, and then he had gone into the kitchen to fix himself a bowl of cereal for breakfast. When I passed through the kitchen on the way to the laundry room, he asked me if Nikki was up yet. I told him that she was having her morning nap. He was about to ask me something else when Vivian appears, fully dressed, carrying a bundle of laundry, including her bed linen. 'I decided it might be better if I bathe later in the day,' she said."

"Do you know what she meant by that?"

"No idea. But I can tell you, I don't think she stopped smoking in the house even though I never caught her at it again. But on Thursdays when I did my cleaning, in her room, I would sometimes pick up a Coke can that had a wet cigarette butt in it. When I asked her about them, she said that a friend of hers sometimes had a smoke outside if the weather was nice. But I wondered about that. Why would someone bring a can with a cigarette butt in it back upstairs when the recycle bin is right there by the back door?

"That same Monday she slipped a Coke can into the recycle bin, I looked in it. It didn't have cigarette butt. Good thing, too. If it had, I would have told Mrs. Zamborska."

"You don't like her very much, do you?"

"Connor, I take a lot of pride in my work. I only work for people I like and who like me. This one— this child—thought that I worked for her. She tried to tell me about the way they do things in English households. From what she described, I can tell you I've seen the same movies she has."

"Did you ever see her mistreat Nikki?"

"No. Can't say that I did."

Yolanda let out a sigh, and I knew our conversation was over. It was the end of her day, and she needed the rest of the bus ride to let some quiet settle in. She didn't want or need any more conversation.

We were almost to Yolanda's stop when it occurred to me that the bus driver would demand another fare for my ride back to Tower Hill Road. I sure didn't want to ask Yolanda again, so I decided to get off in Old Town and walk to Margaret's. She would drive me home or give me money for the bus fare.

Yolanda's stop was one before Margaret's. I thanked

her and told her I'd be by the Farkases' tomorrow afternoon to repay her.

"I'll be at your house on Friday. Why don't you just have your mother include it with my check?"

I liked it that she didn't protest and say, "That's all right," or "Forget about it," or, "Don't worry about it." That was Yolanda's way. Calm. Smooth. One thing at a time.

16.

Margaret's business hours were over, so I went around to the back of the house. The lights were on in the living room, and I saw her sitting in a chair. The TV wasn't on. She was just sitting there, holding a glass of wine. I knocked.

"I was expecting you," she said. "Would have been disappointed if you hadn't shown up."

"How come?"

"Your mother called. She said that you had called her to say that you would be late. Then she happened to look outside when Yolanda boarded the bus, and what should she see but you sitting there, ready to ride the bus downtown. She assumed you were coming to see me, but she was curious about why you didn't get off at home."

"I had to talk to Yolanda. Branwell wanted me to."

"I'd like to hear all about it. What do you think will happen if you call your mother and tell her that you and I are going out for dinner?"

"I think it'll be fine after I explain about the bus." As I picked up the phone, I said, "This might be a long conversation."

"I'll listen as you speak. It'll save a replay."

We went to the One-Potato for supper. We had to wait to be seated. They give you a number and a little remote to hold, and when your number comes up, the remote vibrates to let you know your table is ready. Margaret and I had a booth, which I liked a lot because I wasn't too eager for anyone to overhear what we had to say. Our server came over and introduced herself (she was Tammi, just as it said on her badge) and asked how were we doing this evening and what could she get us to drink. Margaret put our dinner orders in with our drink orders because she wanted Tammi to interrupt as little as possible.

I told Margaret that I didn't use the BATHROOM card, after all, and that Branwell had spelled out Yolanda, and for the first time I felt that his silence had changed. That—as strange as it may sound— Branwell was less accepting of it.

Since Branwell's silence, I've thought a lot about listening, and I've decided it is an art. Just as our English teacher told us you can put too many adverbs and adjectives into a sentence—it's called overwriting—you can put too many meanings into a statement. I call it over-listening. My mother sometimes does that.

For that reason, I'd never told my mother as much as I'd told Margaret about my involvement in this situation with Branwell. Although my mother—having a master's degree in psychology and working on her doctorate—is a trained listener, she sometimes over-listens, especially when it comes to me. For the sake of my self-image, my mother takes everything—*everything*—I say very seriously.

This is an example of how over-listening works. Suppose I told my mother that today when I saw Branwell, I had the feeling that his silence had changed, that it was more active, she would ask, "Why do you think that?" Now, the point is that I'm not sure I *thought* it. I *felt* it. So I wouldn't really have an answer, but I would feel an obligation to explain, and I would probably describe the whole scene to her, and then to make her understand the difference between today and the other days, I would have to describe the other days, and she would have questions for each step along the way, and I would have been talking for ten minutes and still never really have found a reason for something that was only a feeling.

I never said any of this to Margaret because she is only too ready to find fault with my mother, but she knows that sometimes there are feelings without reasons. Hadn't she told me that she had lied to Vivian because she *felt* like it?

This is what she said when I told her that Branwell's silence had changed. She said, "I think we're circling the bull's-eye." And when I told her that the word *shame* had sprung—full-blown—from my head, and I had decided not to use the BATHROOM card after all, she asked, "What would you say is the difference between embarrass and shame?"

I thought a long time before I answered. "Embarrass is something that makes you feel silly or awkward or out-of-place in the presence of someone else. Shame is something that happens to you on the inside and you don't want anyone else present. Embarrass makes you blush, but shame makes you angry."

"So when you teased Branwell about walking in on Vivian Shawcurt the first time, he blushed. He blushed even more when you mentioned the second time."

"Yeah. But it doesn't take much to make Branwell blush."

"But when you mentioned the third time, he went into a rage."

"That's probably why the word *shame* came popping into my head."

"I'd say you have good instincts."

"What do you think happened in that bathroom?"

"Probably the same thing you do. Think about Vivian and how you felt lighting her cigarettes for her. . . ."

I suddenly wanted this conversation to be over. If I had had bus fare, I would have walked out of the One-Potato right then and there.

". . . then remember that Branwell had had a much larger dose of Vivian's charms than you ever did, so try to put yourself into 198 Tower Hill Road on October twelfth . . ."

I said nothing.

". . . after Yolanda leaves . . ."

I simmered.

". . . and Vivian suddenly remembers that she hasn't had her morning bath."

I decided not to speak to Margaret for the rest of the night, maybe for the rest of my life.

Margaret finished eating in silence (thank goodness). Then Tammi brought the check. Margaret looked over the bill, took a credit card from her wallet, and slipped it into the leather folder. She folded her hands on the table and stared at me until I looked back at her. "So!" she said. "Considering how you've clammed up since I mentioned Vivian, I think we can agree that shame leads to withdrawal and anger."

Despite myself, I answered. "What am I, Margaret, your test case against Vivian Shawcurt?"

"More like a textbook case."

"Of what?"

"Of adolescent infatuation."

"I am not an adolescent."

"Yes, you are. Somewhere between youth and grown-up is adolescence. You've done a lot of growing up in the weeks since Branwell was struck dumb. And you're growing in the right direction."

Tammi returned with the charge slip. Margaret added the tip and signed, took the yellow copy, put it in her purse, closed her purse, and asked, "What are you going to do next?"

"Go home. It's a school night. Are you going to drive me?"

"Sure. Let's go."

We were in the car, and Margaret had already pulled

out of the parking lot of the One-Potato before I said, "You may be very clever about embarrassing me, Margaret—"

"But only you can shame yourself."

"That may be true, Margaret. I may be ashamed of what I've been thinking about Vivian, and I can pretty much imagine what happened at Branwell's house on Columbus Day, but that is not why he can't talk."

"I think you're right."

"Not talking about something you're ashamed of is not the same thing as being struck dumb. Something else had to have happened. Branwell's silence is something more than not talking. Between Columbus Day and that 911 call, something else happened."

"Let's think about how we can find out. We can't count on The Ancestors—they've left town—or Dr. Zamborska or Tina—they don't know how. That, more or less, leaves Morris Ditmer. Or Branwell. We can wait for Branwell to tell us. But I don't think he will be ready to tell us until he's ready to talk."

"When do you think that will be?"

"I think that depends on Nikki."

As I was getting out of the car, Margaret asked me whether I would be allowed to join her for dinner for a second night in a row.

My mother is basically a very understanding person. There are times when I think that Margaret would find it easier to dislike her if she were not. Margaret will never admit it, and I will never expect her to, but she knows that my mother understands how she felt all those years ago when my mother and my dad got married.

"I'll be there," I said.

"Come early. We'll order in. Pizza from JJ's."

17.

If you were to ask me how I performed in school the day after my round-robin bus rides, I would have to say that there was not much difference between my vegetative state and Nikki's. My eyes were open, but I was not having much interaction with my environment. Christmas was less than two weeks away. And that was good news and bad news. Good news because it meant a break from school. Bad news because we were approaching The Week From Hell. I think every teacher at Knightsbridge signs a pledge to schedule an important test the week before the Christmas recess so that families that plan a winter vacation won't take off early.

* * *

When I stood at the reception desk to have my backpack examined, the woman said, "I think you're the best kind of friend."

"Really?" I said. I do like compliments, but I modestly added, "I'm just doing what any friend would do."

"I don't see anyone else coming here every day like you." After I signed in, she pulled the registration book back. "Maybe I shouldn't be telling you this, but the upstairs night guard, when he comes off duty this morning, he tells me that your friend did not have a good night. Didn't sleep at all. Just sat up and stared at the wall like he was in a coma or something. It's a good thing you come. The day guard thinks your visits cheer him up."

"Did anyone come after me last night?"

"Last evening, after you left, Dr. Zamborska came in with that lawyer, that nice Ms. Gretchen Silver. She comes here often. Has a lot of kids' cases, but she hadn't been in here to see Branwell for at least a week."

"Neither one of them knows how to communicate with him. What do you think upset him?"

"Something he read." She tapped the packet of flash cards. "You know that your friend can read. Ms. Silver, she give your friend some papers, and he read them."

"What kind of papers?"

"From experience I would say the papers were full of what people were saying about Branwell's case. Sort of like evidence. Called depositions."

"Do you know whose depositions?"

"They wouldn't tell me that. They didn't even tell me they was depositions. It was just a guess on my part. What they call an *educated* guess."

"Uh-oh," I said. "I better get up there." Branwell must have read Vivian's deposition.

"What you gonna do?"

"I think I'll tell him about school," I said. "The fact that he's missing it should cheer him up."

"That sounds like a good idea. A good idea from a good friend." I didn't have time to make a modest response. I had to get upstairs.

If the receptionist had not told me that Branwell had not slept last night, I could have guessed. He didn't look too much better than he had the first time I visited him.

"I spoke to Yolanda yesterday," I said. Branwell was still studying his hands. "I don't think Yolanda cared too much for Vivian. That's probably putting it mildly."

He looked up then. But there was a scary blankness in his look. Not quite the zombie-thing, but near enough. He had sunk back deeper into his silence than when I had left him yesterday. "Well, anyway, Yolanda mentioned that Vivian had a bad habit of leaving the door to the bathroom open when she was taking a bath."

Why did I bring that up when I had pledged to myself that I wouldn't? Because when a two-way conversation is one-way, a person will say foolish things just to move air.

I quickly moved on. "Yolanda said that she saw Vivian smoking a cigarette, and Yolanda said she knew that Tina didn't allow any smoking anywhere in the house, especially around the baby." Branwell started watching me, looking at me so hard, you would think he was trying to get inside my head, and, I guess, in a way, he was. "But Yolanda suspects that Vivian smoked in her room anyway. Something about finding cigarette butts in Coca-Cola cans."

Branwell started making frantic motions with his hands as if he were dealing cards. I reached into my backpack and took out the flash cards out, thinking, Oh, no! Not another assignment. But like the good friend the guard said I was, I started laying the cards out—alphabet side up. The guard slipped a notepad on the table without my saying anything to him.

This time Branwell didn't wait for me to point to the letters one at a time. This time, he pointed with his finger. I said them as I wrote them down. "A-G-E-N-C-Y. Agency?" I asked out loud. He blinked twice. "What agency?"

He pointed, and I spelled A-U-P-A-I-R. "The au pair agency?" He blinked twice very rapidly. "You want me to go to the au pair agency?" Blinked twice again. "And tell them what?" He rapidly pointed to the letters that spelled S-M-O-K-E-S. "You want me to go to the au pair agency and tell them that Vivian smokes?" Two blinks. "Why?"

The cards again. S-T-O-P-H-E-R-G-E-T-J-O-B.

I had to work on that a minute until I said, "Stop her getting a job?" He blinked. "You mean, stop her from getting another job?" He blinked again. "Do you know the name of the agency?"

He shook his head no.

"Well," I said, gathering up my cards, "I have some research to do."

It was five o'clock when I got to Schuyler Place. I saw the light on in the front office and knew that Margaret would be finishing up, so I went around back. I dropped my book bag and jacket on the sofa and went into the kitchen to grab a snack. Margaret had laid in a good supply of cheese and fruit and containers of rice pudding. I found a bag of potato chips in the cupboard and helped myself to those and to a Coke.

As soon as Margaret came in, she said, "Let's order our pizza."

"You don't usually eat this early. What's your hurry?"

"You look hungry," she said, eyeing the bag of chips.

"You have another reason."

"I do. If I wait until JJ's gets really busy, we'll have to take whatever delivery person is available for Schuyler Place, and I want Morris." She called JJ's, and I heard her ask for him. Pause. "I would appreciate it if you can arrange it." Pause. "Yes, Morris Ditmer." Pause. "Yes." Pause. "I owe him some change and a tip." She hung up and asked, "Did you see Branwell today?"

The bad news was that he seemed to have sunk deeper into his silence. The good news was for the first time, he had pointed to the letters himself. I told her that the conversation—if you want to call it that—went much faster when he did the pointing instead of me.

Margaret began raiding the refrigerator for salad in-gredients, and I started to set the table. As I opened the silverware drawer, I remembered how Margaret had lied to Vivian about changing the silverware.

Margaret had lied and had known that I wouldn't contradict her. How had she known? I guess she knew that I wouldn't embarrass her in front of another person. I would never do that. And, I guess, she also knew that I would know that if she was lying, she had a reason for it.

"Margaret," I said, "when you lied to Vivian about changing the silverware drawer, you said you did it because you felt like it. Then when you said that you knew that Morris was lying about never having seen Branwell, you told me that people lie for only one reason—fear. When you lied to JJ's just now telling them that you owed Morris money, were you lying for fear or because you felt like it?"

"Closer to I felt like it. I think I would call what I did when Vivian was here and what I did just now artful lies. Lies to get at the truth."

"I can think of a time when a person lies out of a sense of courage instead of fear. Like when a soldier is caught behind enemy lines and lies when he says he doesn't know anything. That takes courage."

"You're right. Lying to protect someone does take courage."

"Do you think Morris was lying to protect someone?"

"Maybe that information will be delivered with the pizza."

The doorbell rang, and sure enough there was Morris Ditmer, large square box in hand. "Oh, hi," he said, making no effort to pretend that he didn't recognize Margaret or me.

"Do you have a minute?" Margaret asked.

He walked into the kitchen, turned one of the chairs around, and sat down backwards. Leaning his hands on the back of the chair and his chin on his hands, he said, "Sure."

Margaret said, "Connor and I were wondering if you could give us some information."

"Like what?"

"Like that Wednesday when they made the 911 call, that wasn't the first time you were in the house, was it?"

"That'd be a good guess." Morris reached into his jacket pocket and took out his pack of cigarettes. "Mind if I smoke?" Margaret opened the cupboard and handed him a saucer. He placed it on the table in back of him. "Thanks," he said. He studied his pack of cigarettes for a minute. It was new. He toyed with the little red strip that opens the pack before slipping it back into his pocket.

Margaret stood facing the cupboard for a minute. Then she asked, "Do you mind telling me when you first start seeing Vivian?"

"I don't mind at all," he said. He reached for his cigarettes again. He took one this time, tapped it on the back of his hand before lighting it. With the cigarette dangling from his lips, his right eye squinting, he blew out the match and delicately placed it in the saucer before taking a deep drag and blowing the smoke toward the kitchen ceiling. Then he got up, turned his chair around, sat down again, put the saucer in his lap, took another drag on his cigarette, and studied Margaret, enjoying the attention. "That couple she works for called and told her that they were going to be late. They asked her to please take care of supper. She called and ordered a pizza."

"Do you remember when that was?"

"Not exactly."

"Was it Columbus Day?"

"No. Before that." He smiled to himself. "By Columbus Day, our afternoon meetings were something of a habit. I usually came after she put the baby down for a nap. You see, I don't start work until four-thirty."

"Were you there on Columbus Day?"

"I was. Columbus Day was another American holiday that Vivian didn't know squat about. She's a Brit, you know, and won't let you forget it. So comes Columbus Day, and there I am on my cycle, pulling around to the back, parking there by the back patio, like always, opening the kitchen door like always, and imagine my surprise when this tall, redheaded kid comes into the kitchen from the room off to the side there. I'm wondering if maybe I have entered the wrong house. 'Is Vivian here?' I ask. He was very polite. 'Yes,' he says. 'She's not available at the moment. Would you care to come in and wait?' I say, 'No, thank you,' and he says, '*Whom* may I say is calling?' Whom may I say is calling. 'Just tell her that Morris stopped by,' I say, and I start out the door."

"Next thing I know, Vivian is rushing downstairs, calling to me to wait. I do. She invites me into the living room, and the kid follows. Vivian says to him, 'Don't you have homework or something, Branwell?' The kid looks embarrassed, and says, 'Yes, I do.' Then he looks over at me and asks to be excused. It's his frickin' house, and he asks me if he can be excused. He leaves the room and heads off toward the kitchen. Yeah. I was there. That was the first time I seen the Branwell kid."

"But something changed after Columbus Day?"

"Sorta. After that, Vivi told me to carry a pizza box whenever I came. Even if it was empty. I was supposed to pretend I was delivering but only if one or the other of the Doctor Zamborskas was at home, but if it was only Branwell, I didn't have to worry."

"Why was that?"

"Dunno." He shrugged and reached his arms over the back of the chair. "I just remember that Vivi said that if Branwell was there, we could pretend he wasn't."

"Do you know why?"

Morris shrugged. "Dunno. Your guess or the kid here, his guess is as good as mine."

I didn't like being "the kid here." Then Margaret did the kindest thing. She turned the questioning over to "the kid." She said, "Connor, is there something you want to ask Morris?"

"Was Nikki ever awake when you came to the house?"

"We always waited until it was time for her to take a nap. Sometimes, she would not be quite asleep when I come, and sometimes she would start to wake up before I left, but after that Columbus Day, Branwell always took care of her when he come home from school. He'd come home about four,

four-fifteen. He'd go straight upstairs to the nursery."

I swallowed hard. "So that Wednesday was not the first time you were in Vivi's room when Branwell came home?"

"Right. I was usually on my way out when he come home, but after Vivian told me not to worry, I didn't. Sometimes, I'd be going out the back door as he was coming in the front. If he saw me, he never said so. Vivian, she told me he wouldn't say nothing. So I sometimes said 'hi' or 'bye,' but he never answered back. It was like Vivi said, like he wasn't there. A few times, Vivi and me would still be in the room, but he never come in. Never said a word. Just went up to the nursery, and if the baby was up, we would hear him saying sweet things to her as he changed her diaper."

"Her *nappy*," Margaret said sarcastically.

"Yeah, that's what Vivi calls 'em. The only thing different that Wednesday was that Branwell come home early, and Vivian, being a Brit, as she likes to tell me, didn't know about the school Thanksgiving holiday starting with early dismissal on Wednesday. She don't know anything about American holidays."

"And proud of it," Margaret said.

"I think you're right about that."

"What do you think really happened?"

"I . . . I . . ." He took a deep drag on his cigarette, squinted his right eye as he exhaled. The smoke rose toward the ceiling, and he lifted his chin to follow it, then sat like that with his chin up until he suddenly lowered his head and studied his cigarette as he drubbed it out. "I . . . I dunno," he said at last. Then, holding the saucer in one hand and the cigarette in the other, he pressed on the stub until it bent, then broke, and squiggles of tobacco poked out of the paper wrapper. "Well," he said, "I gotta get back to JJ's. There's probably a stack of orders waiting for me to deliver." Margaret checked the bill that was taped to the top of the box, took a ten-dollar bill out of her wallet, and handed it to Morris. He started to reach into his pocket for change, and she waved him off. He said thanks, and I thought he would leave, but he hung back. "How's that baby doin'?" he asked.

"She is in a vegetative state," I answered.

"But she'll come out of it, won't she?"

"Dunno," I said.

As Morris turned to go, Margaret said, "We'll be happy to keep you posted. How can we get in touch with you? Are you in the phone book?"

"No. I have roommates. The phone's under one of their names."

"Can we call you at JJ's?" Margaret asked.

"Not unless you're ordering pizza."

"I can't keep calling for pizzas."

"Then send a fax."

Margaret smiled. "I just may do that," she said.

18.

No sooner had Morris closed the door than Margaret said, "Let's eat."

We each pulled a slice of pizza out of the box, and I said, "I think Morris is lying when he says that he doesn't know what happened that Wednesday."

Margaret took a big bite of pizza and chewed and chewed before she said, "There's something he's not telling us, that's for sure. Do you think he is lying out of fear or courage? Do you think he's protecting Vivian?"

I said, "Dunno. I keep thinking about how Morris had been a regular visitor to Tower Hill Road and Branwell saw him quite a few times but never said anything about him. It was like he started his silence then. I think Branwell's silence about Morris is linked to his silence now."

"Probably," Margaret said.

"There was a day—the day that The Ancestors visited Branwell—remember I said I thought that by not saying anything, Branwell could not say the wrong thing, and I knew it was important not to say the wrong thing to Big Beacham. Remember I said that that particular day, I thought that Branwell's silence was a weapon."

Almost to herself, Margaret said, "A silent weapon." Then she said, "Yes, Connor, I do believe that this silence—his muteness—is a weapon. And it may be a weapon of defense. Or it may be a weapon of aggression. But there was that other silence." Then she asked me something like one of the questions Branwell would ask. A question like *if a tree falls in a forest.* This is what Margaret asked: "Have you ever heard the saying 'The cruelest lies are often told in silence'?"

"Who said it?"

"A lot of people have said it, but Robert Louis Stevenson said it first."

"Are you saying that Branwell's silence is a lie?"

"*Was* a lie. I'm referring to the silence before that 911 call. *That* silence was a lie. Branwell knows that he should have said something to Tina and Dr. Zamborska about Vivian's entertaining Morris when she was supposed to be watching the baby. From Columbus Day to the day he made that 911, Branwell told a cruel lie in silence.

"It's no wonder he had a sleepless night when he read Vivian's deposition. I'm sure there were in her deposition some of the same things that she had said to you and me at dinner. Plus all the lies she told in silence. I'm sure she did not mention Morris Ditmer at all. Branwell must have been up all night trying to think of ways to stop her from getting another job as an au pair. So when you mentioned that Morris said that she had started smoking again, it occurred to him that smoking in the house and lying about it would be the way for him to do it without having to mention certain other things. I guess that's when he thought of Yolanda. She could testify about Vivian's smoking."

Margaret asked me if I could remember *exactly* what Morris had said about Vivian's worry about the agency and smoking. "And don't tell me *dunno*."

"Morris said she was worried about her career, and I asked what career, and he said, 'Her career as an au pair.'"

"And?"

"And he said that she said that the agency won't place her if they find out, and I asked, 'Find out what?' and he said, 'Someone might tell them that she started smoking again.' And then he looked directly at me—slyly—meaning that she was worried that I might tell the agency that she started smoking again. He said that she's back to smoking to soothe her nerves."

"What's the name of the agency?"

"Dunno," I answered.

Margaret asked, "Is that a disease you've caught?"

"Dunno."

Usually when Margaret drove me home, she would stop the car, keep her foot on the brake until I got out, then wave good-bye as soon as she saw me enter the house. But that evening, she pulled into our driveway and cut the motor. She rested her arms on the steering wheel, thinking.

I asked, "Do you think that smoking in the bathroom with the nursery door open is serious enough to keep Vivian from getting another job?"

"I'm not so sure, Connor. We only have Yolanda's word that she caught her smoking. Once. And the fact is, the Zamborskas never complained."

"What do you intend to do?"

"Is your father home?"

"Yes, so is yours."

"I'd like to talk to him."

I got out of the car, ran around to the driver's side, opened her door, and said, "Be my guest."

It was funny, but this time when Margaret referred to him as father, she wanted to talk to him about being the registrar. She wanted to know the rules about au pairs. Without either of them mentioning names, Dad knew who Margaret was talking about. Dad is like that: He doesn't ask unnecessary questions.

Dad did know all the rules about visas and work permits and green cards, because when students and researchers come to the university from foreign countries, they need one or another of them. For example, Dad explained, if someone comes from England to do research at the university or to be a visiting professor, that researcher or professor has to prove that they are so outstanding that no one else can do what they do, and they are not taking a job away from anyone who is a U.S. citizen.

"Does an au pair need a green card?" Margaret asked.

Dad said they don't. Au pairs come into the country under a J-1 Exchange Visitors visa, which is good for twelve months on the condition that the au pair meets all her responsibilities to the host family, does not accept paid employment outside of the family, and returns home at the end of her stay.

He also knew about the agency that had placed Vivian with the Zamborskas. It was the Summerhill Agency in London. Dad said he worked with them in placing au pairs and nannies with lots of university families. The Summerhill Agency screens all their clients. To be placed by them, a person must be courteous, considerate, and respectful to the host family, must obey all the U.S. laws about drugs and alcohol, and must be a nonsmoker or be willing to stop smoking.

Margaret wanted to know what happens when an au pair leaves her host family before her time is up. Dad said, "Summerhill will attempt to find her another placement."

I asked, "Will the Summerhill Agency find her another place if they know that she didn't keep her promise to stop smoking?"

Dad answered my question very seriously. "That would probably depend upon what the first host family had to say. For example—and this is just an example—if the Zamborskas said that Vivian was wonderful in every way except for her smoking, Summerhill would probably give her a reprimand and then extract another promise from her to stop."

"What happens if the au pair does not go to another host family?"

"In that case," Dad said, "Summerhill will inform the United States Immigration and Naturalization Service. Her visa will be canceled, and she will have to leave the country immediately or be deported." He smiled at Margaret and asked if there was anything else she needed to know.

"Summerhill's address."

"Coming right up," Dad said as he checked his Rolodex. He wrote Summerhill's address, phone and fax numbers on a Post-it and handed it to Margaret.

She thanked him and told him that before she faxed the letter to Summerhill, she would like him to look it over. Dad said that it would be a privilege to help in any way he could. He looked at his watch, and I caught Margaret's eyebrows go skyward with a look of disapproval. (She accuses Dad of running his life with a stopwatch. "He is the only man in the world," she has said, "whose excuse for never going to a McDonald's is because they don't take reservations.") Imagine her surprise when the next words out of

Dad's mouth were, "No rush, Margaret Rose." (She loves it when he calls her Margaret Rose.) "It's eight-thirty here. That means it's already early Saturday morning in London. Summerhill offices are closed until nine A.M. Monday, Greenwich Mean Time."

Margaret said, "Well, Dad" (He loves it when she calls him Dad.), "I'll just have to get the wires humming early." They didn't hug or kiss when they said good night, but the air between them was gentle.

19.

Nikki had been out of a coma for two weeks now, but these vegetative days seemed harder than all the others. Waiting takes up a lot more energy than people give it credit for. Say you are sitting in a theater; knowing there is a lot of stuff going to happen behind the curtain, but the curtain is stuck and can't go up; I give waiting for the curtain to go up a *three*. Say you are late for a soccer game, and your mother has to stop for a red light, and the line of cars in front of her is so long, she has to wait for a second green before she can go; I give waiting for the second light a *five*. Say you are in math class waiting for the teacher to hand back the results of a test that you had not studied for; I give waiting for the test results a *ten*. Waiting for something to begin is harder than waiting for something to end, so I give waiting for Nikki to track a *twelve*.

In the movies, coming out of the vegetative state is very sudden and very glamorous. I don't know how many movies I have seen when the actor-patient suddenly blinks his or her eyes and then opens them and starts to talk. "Where am I?" or "What happened?" or "What day is this?" And there is always a kindly doctor plus the patient's loved ones there to say, "You've been in an accident." And if patients have tubes in them, they're in their arms, where they don't interfere with things such as tender kisses or makeup.

So much for Hollywood.

Most days I gave waiting for Branwell to speak a *four-plus*. Some days, a *five*. At least I had a way of communicating that got responses. It was not like I was bowling and was not allowed to see how many pins I knocked down. My investigation was showing results.

I told Branwell that Margaret was preparing a letter to fax to the Summerhill Agency. I also told him that my father had confirmed that any au pair that was placed by them must be a nonsmoker or be willing to stop smoking. Then I made the mistake of telling him that my father had also said that if the Zamborskas said that she was wonderful in every way except for smoking, Summerhill will find Vivian another family. She would just have to make another promise to stop.

As soon as he heard me say that the Summerhill Agency might still find Vivian another family, I got quite a reaction. He didn't turn over his chair, but he started motioning with his hands so frantically that I got a windchill. He wanted me to deal the cards.

It's probably a good thing that he was anxious, because I wasn't. This was the last weekend before The Week From Hell. I didn't want another assignment— which is what I had intended to tell him when I arrived. I intended to tell him to ease up, but considering his fury, I was not about to resist one little bit.

But I didn't have to like it.

I dutifully pulled the cards out of my backpack. They were getting a little dog-eared now. I laid them out so that the names showed. Branwell made a flipping motion with his hands. I sighed heavily so that it would be clear to him how tired I was of doing this (at this particular time). I guess he got the hint, but instead of letting me off the hook, he started turning the cards over himself. I felt a little bad about that but not too bad.

I took out the notepad that the guard had given me, and dug around in the bottom of my backpack until I came up with a pencil that didn't have a broken tip. I dutifully started pointing to the letters, but Bran brushed my pencil aside and pointed to the letters himself. This did nothing to help me feel appreciated.

I kept my voice level as I called out the first of the letters he pointed to, but I wouldn't write it down until he blinked. He waited for me to write it down, and I waited for him to blink. He wouldn't blink, and I wouldn't write. He waited, and I waited. He blinked. He pointed to the next letter, and we played the same wait-and-wait game. Finally, he blinked again. With neither of us saying a word, we were having an argument.

T-E-L-L-S-U-M-M-E-R-H-

"Tell Summerhill?" He blinked. "Tell them what?"

V-I-V-I-

"Vivian?" He blinked. "Vivian what?"

N-O-T-K-E-E-P-P-R-O-M-I-S-

"All right," I said, "I'll have Margaret put in the letter that Vivian will not keep her promise not to smoke."

I started gathering up the cards (again), and (again) he wouldn't let me. He pulled them out of my hand

and laid them back out on the table. He began pointing, pointing, pointing, so rapidly that before I could
wait for him to blink as I called it out, he pointed to
another so that it was not necessary to wait for him to
blink after each of the letters.

P-H-O-N-E-S-U-M-M-E-

"You want me to phone Summerhill?"

Much to my annoyance, he shook his head no, and
began pointing to letters again. I wondered if that
woman who wrote a whole book with the guy who
could only blink his left eye ever had a week of exams
coming up.

M-A-R-G-A-

"You want me to have Margaret call?" He blinked
twice.

C-A-L-L-N-O-W-U-R-G-E-N-T.

"Call now?" He blinked, then pointed to where I had
written URGENT. "Listen, Branwell, the Summerhill
Agency is not open now, so there is no point in having
Margaret call. She'll send them a fax so that they get it
first thing Monday morning. It's better to have these
things in writing, anyway. Margaret says that you
never know who you're going to get on the phone,
and most of the time, you get voice mail."

Branwell was really agitated. He pointed again to
URGENT.

I looked at the clock on the wall. "Listen, Branwell, I told you the Summerhill office is closed today and tomorrow. They certainly won't be getting Vivian another job between now and then. I'll have Margaret make sure they get her letter at nine A.M., Monday morning."

He shook his head sadly and pointed again to URGENT.

I felt a strong need to tell him that I had urgent needs of my own. I don't know what was wrong with me. I'm not proud of the fact that I felt the need to be more appreciated. And I'm not proud of the fact that I felt the need to tell him that I was facing The Week From Hell and that we had a lot of after-school rehearsals for our Holiday Concert. I guess in my heart I knew that Branwell appreciated me, but I got the feeling that he thought he was doing me a favor by letting me in the game.

SIAS: Waiting for Branwell to speak is a *twelve point five.*

20.

Margaret faxed the letter to Dad early on Sunday. As soon as he read it, he picked up the phone and called her. Much to my surprise, he didn't have to look up her number.

I heard him say, "You've done an excellent job, Margaret Rose." He held the letter in front of him and looked it over as he listened. Then I heard him say, "Yes, very professional." Then, "Yes," and another, "Yes," and then, "No trouble at all," and, "Keep me posted."

After Dad hung up, I asked if Margaret would be sending the letter now since she had gotten his approval. He said that she planned on sending it out first thing on Monday morning.

"Our first thing or London's first thing?" I asked. And then I mentioned that I had promised Branwell that Margaret would fax the letter to London so that Summerhill would have it when they opened their offices on Monday morning.

Dad reminded me that London is five hours ahead of Epiphany, New York because London and all of England is on Greenwich Mean Time. "That means that if Margaret wanted to fax them at nine o'clock in the morning GMT, she would have to do it at 4:00 A.M. Eastern Standard Time, and I do not think it would be prudent to ask someone to stay up or get up at four o'clock in the morning just to fax a letter to London."

Prudent is a Republican word that Dad's second-favorite living president used a lot. It means to be careful about one's conduct. Considering that Margaret is a lifelong Democrat, and that Dad is the other, and further considering that Dad and Margaret Rose seemed to be getting along pretty well lately, I did not think it would be prudent tell her what he said because *prudent* would only remind her of their differences.

Finally, Dad gave me the copy of the letter Margaret had faxed to him.

I read the following:

Ms. Louisa Hutchins, Director
Summerhill Infant and Child Care Agency
1407 Dalton Lane
London WC 1X8LR
ENGLAND

Dear Ms. Hutchins:

It has come to my attention that Ms. Vivian Shawcurt, whom your agency placed as an au pair in the household of Drs. Stefan and Tina Zamborska, has left that household. The infant Nicole Zamborska, who was in her care, is hospitalized as a result of a nonaccidental head injury. An investigation into the cause of that injury is pending.

As the bargaining representative for Ms. Vivian Shawcurt, Summerhill Infant and Child Care Agency is hereby requested to provide documentation showing either that she has found alternate placement or that she has returned to England. If such verification cannot be produced, then we must conclude that Ms. Shawcurt has not fulfilled the responsibilities of her assignment and is in violation of the terms of the J-1 Exchange Visitors visa under which she entered the United States. Such notice will be sent to the United States Immigration and Naturalization Service.

Sincerely,

Margaret Rose Kane

I was shocked.
I did not think it was excellent.

I did not think it was "very professional."

It was terrible.

It would not be prudent to send it.

This "excellent" so-called "very professional" letter said nothing at all about Vivian's smoking. After all the investigating I did with Yolanda and after I had lit not just one but several of Vivian's cigarettes, which made me an eyewitness to her broken promise to quit smoking.

I went into the kitchen to make a phone call. I wanted to speak where Dad could not hear me because I had something to say to Margaret Rose that he did not need to hear. I wanted to tell his daughter that I did not like her letter at all. I did not think it was *excellent*. I did not think it was *very professional*. And I did not think that it would be prudent to send it at 4:00 A.M. Eastern Standard Time or 9:00 A.M. Greenwich Mean Time or any time. Ever.

I also wanted to tell Margaret Rose that it was not fair to agree with The Registrar about something that involved me without consulting me. Being left out is never nice. Branwell knows that, and Margaret certainly does.

When Margaret answered the phone, I cupped my hand over the mouthpiece and said, "Meet me over The Ditch." And I hung up.

I put on my jacket and left the house without telling anyone where I was going. I took the letter with me.

I walked slowly. I didn't care if Margaret got there first and had to wait. The campus was Sunday-empty, almost silent. As I made my way to the bridge, I wondered how she expected me to show that letter to Branwell.

After all the trouble I had gone to getting Yolanda to tell me about how Vivian had smoked in the house, upstairs where the baby slept, against the expressed wishes of the baby's mother, her letter should at least have mentioned that there were people who had seen that she had broken a serious promise to Summerhill. Morris Ditmer himself said that Vivian was worried that someone might tell them that she started smoking again. He had looked right at me when he had said it.

Well, I wasn't silent to the bone like Branwell. I was ready to give a deposition about her smoking.

I was on the bridge over the gorge and, out of habit, I began looking for lovers. I didn't see any. I remembered the last time I had stopped on the bridge. I leaned my elbows on the bridge railing and wondered when I would ever have someone to take a walk with. Vivian was out of the question now. I still had the butterfly hair grip in my sock drawer at home. (My mother refuses to pair my socks or turn them right side out, so she just dumps them in the drawer. I sometimes have mismatched socks, but the drawer is my best hiding place for small things like barrettes.)

I hoped the store would let me take the barrette back, because it seemed I wouldn't be able to give it to her. For one thing, I didn't know where she was. Who did? I didn't. Margaret didn't. Dad didn't. It would be a good guess that the Zamborskas didn't know, either. Summerhill would be the most logical place to find her. And if the Summerhill Agency doesn't know where she is . . . if Summerhill doesn't know, then Vivian is in trouble. In trouble with her J-1 Visa. Big time.

And then I read the letter again.

Of course.

My seeing Vivian smoke was not proof that she had not quit during the time she had been with the Zamborskas.

The cigarette butts that Yolanda found in the Coke cans could have been put in while Vivian was outside the house, or they could have been put there by someone else. That evidence was only circumstantial, and the rest was Yolanda's word against Vivian's.

Now that my head was static free, I heard my

conversation with Morris Ditmer loud and clear.

"Vivi, she's real worried."

"Is she worried that Branwell will be able to speak and tell the agency that Nikki was breathing funny when he found her?"

"Nah. Vivi's not worried about anything Branwell might say."

"So what is she worried about?"

"Her career."

"What career?"

"As an au pair. She says that the agency won't place her if they find out."

"Find out what?"

"Someone might tell them that she's started in smoking again. She don't look it, but she's real high-strung, and with all that's happened, she's back to smoking to soothe her nerves."

The clues were in the verbs. All the verbs about Vivi were in the present tense.

Morris knew where Vivian was.

Dad was right. Margaret had written an excellent letter. Very professional. She had really written the letter for Morris Ditmer. He knew where Vivian Shawcurt was, and where she was, was with him.

* * *

I saw Margaret down at the far end of the bridge. I started walking toward her as she walked toward me. By the time we met in the middle, I was wearing a smile as wide as the gorge, and I said, "Did you fax it to him?"

"This morning."

"Have you heard from him?"

"JJ's doesn't open until eleven."

"What do you think he's going to do?"

"He's going to try to stay out of trouble."

"That was a good letter."

"Thank you. Did you always think so?"

"No." We started walking toward Old Town. I decided to continue across campus to get to the Behavioral Center. "Did you tell Dad that you suspected that Vivian is with Morris?"

"Not until after he read the letter."

"Is that when he said 'very professional'?"

"As a matter-of-fact, it was."

"Are you even going to fax a copy to Summerhill?"

"Of course I am. I wouldn't lie to you or Branwell."

"At least not about that."

I followed Branwell's eyes as he skimmed the letter very quickly, then returned to the top and read it slowly, line by line. I told him that Margaret would be faxing it to London first thing Monday morning.

Bran laid the letter on the table, turned, so that I could read it right-side-up. He pointed to the part of the letter about her finding alternate placement or returning to England. I read the whole line out loud. "So?" I said. "No one knows where she is. She seems to have disappeared after giving her deposition."

Branwell got extremely nervous. He put his finger on the words *alternate placement* and rubbed it back and forth until the ink was smudged, the whole time shaking his head no. He was on the verge of tears. He rubbed his eyes in an effort to keep the tears from falling, and some of the ink from his finger rubbed off. "Don't worry," I said. "They'll find her." I felt bad that I had to leave the real purpose of the letter unspoken.

Branwell got up and left the room with ten minutes left on our visiting clock.

DAY TWENTY

21.

Monday was the beginning of The Week From Hell. Maybe it was the accumulation of schoolwork that had piled up, maybe these vegetative days of Nikki's were wearing on me more than I thought, maybe it was just the way Branwell had walked out on me yesterday that made me think that he didn't appreciate me, but on that Monday, I really didn't want to give him a chance to give me another assignment. I had enough to do already. So after school, I didn't go directly to the Behavioral Center. I went to Margaret's. I was exhausted. My blood sugar was low. I needed a snack.

I had surveyed the treats cupboard and was hanging out in front of the open refrigerator when Margaret came bursting through the door that leads from her offices. "Nikki smiled!" She was shouting.

I slammed the refrigerator door shut and ran to her as she ran to me, and we hugged each other and did a little foot-stomping dance, laughing, as we circled the kitchen table.

"How did it happen?"

"Tina and the nurse were talking, and Nikki suddenly opened her eyes but closed them right away again. So Tina went over to crib, and said, 'Nikki? Nikki. Mama's here,' and Nikki opened her eyes and smiled at Tina."

"Did this just happen?"

"Don't know. I just found out."

"I can't wait to tell Branwell," I said, running to get my jacket.

"It'll be nice for him to hear it from you."

"I can't wait to see what he does when I tell him it's over—"

"Not so fast."

"It's all going to be all right now, isn't it?"

"Not *all* all right. She's off zero, but she's just arrived at the starting line."

"How long?"

"There's no telling how far she has to go or how fast she will be able to." Margaret saw the look of disappointment on my face. She put an arm across my shoulder and pulled me to her and said, "But it's a start."

"What has to happen next?"

"She has to track."

"Aren't we there yet?"

"She has to show conscious behavior."

"She smiled. They don't think it was gas, do they? What conscious behavior can an infant have?"

"She can follow an object with her eyes. She can squeeze someone's finger. She can gurgle when delighted." Margaret hesitated, then added, "You'll be sure to tell him that it's not over yet. Be sure that he knows that that the fat lady still hasn't sung."

"Vivian's not fat," I said, smiling. "Shall I tell him you sent the fax to Summerhill?"

"Yeah, tell him. And, Connor?"

"What?"

"Come back after you've seen him. I'd love to know his reaction. I'll drive you home."

When Branwell was brought into the visitors' room, the first words out of my mouth were, "Nikki smiled."

Branwell smiled in return.

I am not like the kids I see at the supermarket who are eating their free cookie with one hand and grabbing Oreos off the shelf with the other. I don't usually want one thing more than I have, but this time, if I am to be perfectly honest (and I've tried to be throughout), I really did want one thing more. Maybe because my blood sugar was low and it was The Week From Hell, I wanted a shout, a sound—any sound. Even a whimper would do.

I told him what Margaret had said about tracking. He listened quietly. Maybe *he* needed the Oreos.

I told him that Margaret had sent the fax, and that from now on, it was wait-and-see time. About Vivian. And about Nikki.

He remained motionless, so I got up to leave. If he could leave when he had had enough, so could I.

SIAS: I was relieved, hungry, and in desperate need of something sweet.

As soon as I got to Margaret's, I started my search for snacks exactly where I had left off—hanging on to the handle of the refrigerator door. I heard a motor running, then cut off. I ran to the back door and saw Morris Ditmer get off his cycle, remove his helmet, and come to the back door. He knocked. I answered.

He pulled a letter out of his pocket. I recognized the letterhead. It was Margaret's.

"I've got to talk to your sister," he said bluntly.

I told him that she closed up shop at five and would be here soon. I invited him to come in and wait. He sat in the chair that I had been sitting in the night that Vivian came for supper. He sat at attention with his helmet under his arm. I asked him if he wanted something to eat or drink, and he said no, so I returned to the kitchen to get some help for my blood sugar, and the whole time he sat there in the living room like a United States Marine if Marines ever wore multiple earrings and pierced their body parts.

When Margaret came in, he stood and handed her the letter. "Did you write this?" he asked.

"I did."

"How illegal is Vivian?" he asked.

"Enough to either be arrested or deported." She sat down on the sofa and asked, "Do you want me to go on?" He nodded. "Officially, she is a fugitive. It is illegal for anyone to knowingly harbor a fugitive."

"What if the person doing the harboring doesn't know this person is a fugitive?"

Margaret shrugged. "I guess that's something the person would have to convince the authorities about."

"Convince them how?"

"Sometimes the authorities make plea bargains if you give them information they need."

Morris laid his helmet at his feet and sank into the chair. "Like what?"

"Like what you know about Vivian and Nikki."

"She says that she didn't hurt the baby."

"I'm sure she does. But you suspect something else, don't you, Morris?" He nodded. "Maybe if you tell us what you witnessed, we can help."

"She says that the brother, that Branwell kid, he was always at her."

"*Her* being the baby or *her* being Vivian."

"Both. I did see that Branwell kid take care of the baby a real lot. Like I told you. He was always changing her whether she needed it or not."

"But that is what Vivian told you, isn't it? You don't know that the baby didn't need changing. As a matter-of-fact, you probably suspect that she did."

"Well, yeah. That part about whether she needed it or not is what Vivi said." He picked up his helmet and began rubbing the chin strap. Back and forth. Back and forth. He studied what he was doing for a long time, then said, "Vivian wasn't always nice to that baby." He took a deep breath. "Like I told you, we always waited until it was time for her to take a nap, but sometimes, we'd be up in Vivi's room and the baby would not be quite asleep. Those times—I mean those times when the baby was not quite asleep, and she would be cranky—well, there were those times when I would hear Vivi go in there and yell at the baby, and if she was laying on her back, she would pop her over onto her tummy. And if she was on her tummy, she would pop her over onto her back and jam a pacifier into her mouth. I actually seen her do that a coupla times. She'd yell at the kid. What good is yelling at a little kid like that, I'd ask. A coupla times I hadda ask her to change the baby's diaper—her nappy—like she called it. It took only one whiff to know what was the matter, but after Columbus Day—that day we talked about—she never did. 'Branwell will be home soon enough,' she'd say. 'He'll do it. Brannie will be only too happy to do it.'"

Margaret asked him if he knew anything more about what had happened to the baby on that Wednesday before Thanksgiving.

"I only know that she told me that the brat—that's what she called her, but I don't know how a baby that little has been around long enough to be a brat—she told me that the brat had been cranky all morning. 'It's been snot and spit all day,' she said. When we got up to the bedroom, the baby was crying. At this point, I had just got there, and we didn't know that Branwell would be home soon, so she went in and changed the diaper. She had pooped in her pants, and it was loose—a real mess. She carried her into the bathroom to change her, and I heard the baby let out a real loud cry, then go quiet. Vivi made some cooing sounds—she could be sweet, you know—and she put the baby into the crib. Then she came on back to the bedroom. She seemed a little upset. I asked her what was the matter. She laughed. 'You can add another s-word to snot and spit.' We had hardly undressed when the kid came home from school, and I heard him yell for Vivian.

"Vivi ran there right away. She was in her bra and panties. I waited there in the bedroom when Vivi she comes running back through the bathroom and tells me to get dressed. She throws on her clothes and goes back into the nursery. I had more clothes to put on than Vivi did because I had finished getting undressed. So I pulled on my clothes and started toward the nursery through that there bathroom. I stopped by the tub, and I seen that there was a spot of blood on the edge of the tub, right by the floor. I took a washrag and wiped it up. Vivi is yelling to the kid to call 911.

He does it, and nothing comes outta his mouth. I come outta the bathroom, and ask what happened, thinking I can help, and Vivi, she just yells at me to go. I went. I was outta there by the time the ambulance come.

"Now, you see, I was telling you the truth when I said that I never seen what happened. I didn't. It still could be that the kid dropped her."

"Morris," Margaret said, "has Vivian threatened you?"

"Not really. She just mentions how I shouldna wiped off that blood. I'm not going to be charged with being an accessory to a crime or anything, am I?"

Margaret said, "Gretchen Silver will know what to do." She told him who Gretchen Silver was and suggested that they try to set up a meeting for the next morning. She told Morris to call her. "I guess I know why you don't want to take any calls from me."

"The same reason I hung up when I made the call."

"Vivian doesn't know that you've talked to Connor or me, does she?"

He looked at Margaret out of the corner of his eye and said, "Miss Kane," he said, "if I had that kind of death wish, I would go straight to Dr. Jack Kevorkian. I wouldn't go sneaking around to the back of your house."

He made us both laugh.

He got up and tucked his helmet under his left armpit. "She was a lot of fun at first. And maybe she could be a lot of fun again. But right now, living with her is like living with that Greek god whose hair is all snakes."

"Medusa?"

"Yeah, that one. That one they say about how she was once beautiful, but she did something wrong and her hair was turned to snakes and every time someone looked at her face they were turned to stone. I'm not stone yet, but I ain't putty anymore, either, and she's working on it." He turned to me and asked, "How did you find me?"

"Well, there was this Frenchman who could only blink his left eye . . ."

"Oh, that guy with the eye in the middle of his forehead?"

"Cyclops."

"Yeah, that one."

"No, this was a Frenchman. It was his left eye."

"A French myth."

"No, it was a memoir."

Margaret interrupted. "I'll let you tell Gretchen Silver your address. I don't want to know it yet."

Morris shook Margaret's hand. I think he would have saluted if he had thought that it would be the right thing to do. He was obviously relieved. Just as he turned to go, he asked, "You're not going to tell any of this to Branwell, are you?"

"Oh," Margaret said. "I think we are. I can't think of anyone who deserves to know it more."

"Yeah," Morris replied. "I guess you're right."

"But we'll tell Gretchen Silver first."

And Morris Ditmer was out the door.

I didn't want to go home. Going home meant hitting the books for the rest of The Week From Hell. I wanted to stay with Margaret and talk about "what ifs," but we both knew where duty lay. I had to get home.

So this is what Margaret did. She gave me her cell phone and set it to vibrate (so that it wouldn't ring in class). If the phone vibrated when I was in class, I was not to answer it, but to check for a message. She showed me how to retrieve messages.

Margaret Rose Kane knows how to make things happen. Or not happen. Whichever.

22.

Margaret was as good as her word. She always was. I checked the cell phone after every class, and finally, just before social studies, I felt a buzz. The message was from Gretchen Silver, who said that as of ten o'clock that morning, Vivian was an illegal immigrant. She could not get work anywhere in the United States and would be deported to England as soon as the paperwork was finished. Margaret has a good sense of timing. I did not ace the social studies test—I never do—but I did well enough.

I had never before had a cell phone in my backpack, and the officer at the receptionist desk played the message before she would allow me to take it up with me. I realized then that Margaret had wisely allowed the message to come from the lawyer. Gretchen Silver had identified herself on the tape so that there would be no question of allowing it in the visitors' room.

The receptionist was curious, and as she put the phone back she asked, "Who is Vivian?"

"Rhymes with rich," I said. That was something that the wife of my father's second favorite living president said. The receptionist knew what I meant, and she laughed.

There was a brighter, better look to Branwell. He came into the visitors' room looking ready. Ready for something. For something new. For anything. I pressed the buttons on the cell phone and handed it to Bran. He held it up to his ear and smiled. He smiled the widest, most real smile I had seen since day one. He handed the phone to me when the message was done. I pressed END, and Bran reached for it again. I pushed the message button and TALK and handed it back to him. He listened again, and pushed END himself and slid the phone across the table. Then he made a motion like he was dealing cards. I dutifully got them out, and put them on the table—alphabet-side out.

Imagine my surprise when he motioned for me to turn them over, and as I did, he laughed. I had turned them all over before I realized that Branwell had laughed. My head sprang up. Branwell had made a sound.

He picked up the card that said BLUE PETER and held it in front of his chest so that the words faced me.

I was speechless. But not for long. "Since when?" I asked.

"Yesterday." That was his answer, and that was the first word he had spoken after three weeks of silence. You could think of *yesterday* as a word with a past, or you could think of it as the title of a Beatles song. Any way you think of it, it was music to my ears.

I asked, "Were you able to speak the day you told me to interview Yolanda?"

"Almost."

"Do you want me to tell anyone?"

"Not yet. Let's wait until Vivian is safely out of the way . . . and . . . and Nikki is. . . "

"Okay, Bran. You don't have to say anything more. I understand."

"I think you do." He leaned across the table toward me (and I swore to myself then and there that if he ever sat too close to me on the bleachers ever again, I wouldn't say a word about it). "I want to tell you everything."

"Do you want me to come back tomorrow?" I asked.

"Sure," he said, "I like to hear about what's happening at day care."

So he had been listening after all.

23.

Over the next two days, my conversations with Branwell were once again only one-way. But the important difference was this: He did the talking, and the first thing he talked about was Columbus Day.

"It was twelve-thirty when Yolanda left for the day, and Nikki was sitting in her carryall, gurgling. Vivian said, half to me and half to Nikki, 'Now it's time for the grown-ups to have lunch.' She made us ham sandwiches—spreading one of the slices of bread with mayonnaise and the other one with mustard. She cut off the crusts, and then cut them into quarters. She laid them out on a platter in a star design. She sliced a pickle and placed the strips like the spokes of a wheel. It all looked so pretty. And so did she as she concentrated on making everything even and nice. We sat opposite each other at the kitchen table, and she told me that she had taken this job because it was near a university, and she told me how much she hoped to become a lawyer. A barrister, she said. Then she asked, 'You don't think I'll look too silly in one of those wigs, do you?'

"I told her that I couldn't think of anything that would make her look silly. I couldn't think of anything except how pretty she was and how she could even make ham sandwiches pretty.

"We finished lunch and cleared the table and loaded the dishwasher. In a way, we did it together. I handed her the dishes, and one by one, she took them from me and slowly—very slowly—put them into the dishwasher. Our fingers touched a couple of times, and when they did, I said, 'Sorry,' and she just smiled shyly.

"This whole time, Nikki was happily playing with her fingers and gurgling, so after the dishwasher was loaded, it seemed like the most natural thing in the world for her to ask me if I would mind bringing Nikki up and putting her in bed when she started to get restless. She said, 'Yolanda insisted that I turn in all the towels, so I haven't had a chance to take my bath. I usually take it while Nikki has her morning nap.' She stopped halfway out the room and said impishly, 'But you know that.'"

"'Yeah,' I said. And I suppose I blushed.

"The first time I walked in on her while she was taking her bath was purely accidental. The second time, I'm not so sure. I try to remember how it happened. I try to remember how I felt."

At this point, Branwell stopped talking. Here he was, getting to the good part, and he stopped to stare into space. I wondered if he needed a prompt. After awhile, he seemed to remember that he could talk, and he said, "I think that second time . . ." Then he shook his head as if to clear it. "That second time, I'm not sure." After another long pause, he said, "I'm not sure it was an accident. I suppose it was a mistake I was waiting to make." Another long pause. "And she knew."

Now it was my turn to blush. Branwell looked at me out of the corner of his eye, and he said, "You know about it, don't you, Connor?"

I swallowed hard and said, "If you're asking me if I've thought about Vivian . . . if you're asking . . . if I dreamed . . ."

He held up his hand. "You don't have to say anymore." He was blushing again, and it was another while before he continued. "I know that after lunch I could hardly wait for Nikki to get fussy. I was tempted to pinch her or something to give me an excuse to pick her up. But, of course, I wouldn't. Finally, Nikki started to get sleepy, so I carried her upstairs in her carryall. I think I knew that I would find the door to the bathroom open. I settled Nikki down. I wouldn't let myself look up at that bathroom door. But I did start the little music box that was at the foot of the crib. I guess I wanted to make sure that Vivian would know that I was up there. I wanted something to happen, but I wanted it to be . . . oh, I don't know . . . I wanted it to be something that was beyond me. Something that just happened, not something that I made happen. Do you understand, Connor?"

I thought of all the dreams I had had about how I was going to find some excuse for seeing Vivian to give her the barrette I had bought for her. That was before I knew she was a *rhymes-with-rich*. (And even sometimes after, I'm ashamed to admit.) I said, "I think I do."

Bran continued, "Well, I looked up at last, and I saw that the bathroom door was open. *Ajar,* I guess is what you would say. It wasn't open wide. I stared at that door a long time, but I didn't move. The little music box wound down, so I wound it up again, and it started to play again. 'Lara's Theme.' Then I heard her call from the bathroom, 'Oh, shoot! I forgot the shampoo.' Then a second later, she called my name. 'Brannie,' she called, 'Brannie, would you be a dear and bring me my shampoo? It's just over there on the vanity. I don't want to traipse water all over the floor. Yolanda will have my head if I do.'

"Well, that was the *beyond-me* I was waiting for. I opened the door to the bathroom, and there she was in the tub, her arms folded crosswise over her breasts. 'Now, don't you be a naughty boy and look,' she said. 'Just reach me that shampoo bottle over there and be on your way.' I walked straight past the tub to the vanity sink and grabbed the bottle of shampoo and held it out to her. I've tried and tried to remember whether she asked me to put the shampoo on the edge of the tub or if she asked me to hand it to her, but I can't. I've tried and tried to remember the order in which things happened next, but I can't.

"I'm not sure what she said or what I said, but I do know that I didn't put the shampoo on the edge of the tub. I handed it to her. She reached for it, and, when she did, I saw . . . I saw her breasts. She laughed and said, 'Oops!' when she realized that . . . that she had . . . that she . . . what she had done, she let the bottle drop into the tub. She quickly leaned forward and grabbed her hands behind her knees. Her head was turned, her cheek resting on her knees, facing me. She said, 'As long as you're here, Brannie, you might as well give the girl's back a scrub.' She reached into the water and handed me the washcloth."

"Did you? Did you wash her back?"

"I did. I washed her back."

"Is that all?"

"Not quite."

"You don't have to tell me the rest."

"Yes, I do. I have to tell you. My father and Gretchen Silver and even—in time—Tina will understand what happened to me, but you, Connor, are the only one who recognizes it."

I remembered when Margaret was telling me about Branwell's first day home after she had picked him up from the airport, and she said that when she saw the look on Branwell's face, she recognized it from her "own personal wardrobe of bad memories," and that was when I knew why Bran had wanted me to start with Margaret. Now he was telling me that I would recognize what had happened to him, and when I thought about lighting Vivian's cigarettes, I knew that I did. I said, "What happened after you washed her back?"

"She stood up and got out of the tub."

"Without shampooing her hair?"

"Without shampooing her hair."

"After she made you bring her the shampoo?"

"I don't think she exactly *made* me bring her the shampoo."

"I think she did."

"She got out of the tub and told me to hand her the bath towel. It would have been an easy reach for her to get it herself, but she wanted me to hold it out for her. I did. And she backed into it, and then—keeping her back to me—she took the two ends of the towel and wrapped them around herself. But she didn't move. She just stood there, her back to my front. And . . . and . . . I kissed her. I kissed her in the curve of her neck where it meets her shoulder, and something happened. A very grown-up thing . . . happened."

"Like a Viagra thing?"

He nodded. "She knew it. She was there, right up against me, and she felt it happen. She turned around and faced me, front to front, with the towel wrapped around her—but not all the way around her—and she said, 'Branwell Zamborska, you are a naughty boy.' I couldn't say anything. I couldn't do anything. Things were happening to me that really were beyond me. She watched and smiled a secret smile.

"I didn't want my father or Tina to know. I didn't want anyone to know. So it became our secret. Except that it became Vivian's secret more than mine. From that day forward, I did whatever she wanted me to do. I took care of Nikki from the minute I came home from school until Dad and Tina came home from work. I did whatever she wanted me to do, and I didn't do what she didn't want me to. I never told them about how I would come home and find Nikki crying with a dirty diaper. I never told them how I would find Vivian with Morris in her room. I never told them about Morris or the smoking or anything. I never said a word.

"And if my father or Tina noticed a difference in me, they never said a word either."

"I did," I said. "I noticed a difference."

"Yes," he said. "I know you did. But don't you think it's funny that my father didn't?"

I didn't answer that. I could have told him that Margaret had said, "I have no doubt that Dr. Zamborska is brilliant, but he is also stupid." But Branwell didn't want me to run his father down any more than Margaret wanted me to razz The Registrar. I thought of telling him about the perfectly carved ivory, but I didn't do that either. This was not the time or the place. Besides, it was Margaret's story. It would be better coming from her.

"You knew all along that something shameful happened on Columbus Day, didn't you?"

"I'm not that smart. I didn't know it all along. I had to figure it out."

I thought it was time to tell Margaret that he could speak.

I told Bran how helpful she had been, and asked him for permission to tell her. He did not reply. He folded his hands on the table in front of him and said nothing. This thinking silence was not empty the way his other silence had been. At last he said, "I knew Margaret would recognize how left out I was, but you can't tell her yet. I cannot leave this place until Nikki leaves the hospital."

"Why?" I asked. "Why?"

Branwell shrugged. "Maybe if I tell you what happened the day I made that 911 call, you'll understand."

This is what he told me.

On the Wednesday before Thanksgiving, he had come home from school to find—as he often had—Morris's motorcycle parked in the back of the house. He went up to Nikki's room immediately, and found her asleep. She had been cranky for the last couple of days. Runny nose. Teething. But when he looked at her, her sleep seemed different. Her breathing was funny. Shallow. She was unresponsive and seemed limp. He tickled her under her chin, but when she opened her eyes, they seemed to roll back in her head. He felt her forehead and thought she felt hot. He picked her up, and she vomited, and her arms extended—rigidly. Branwell knew something was seriously wrong. He called Vivian, and she came running through the Jack-and-Jill. She was in her bra and panties. She took the baby and cleaned the vomit out of her mouth. She started yelling at Branwell. "What have you done?" Then she handed Nikki back to him and rushed back through the bathroom to put on the rest of her clothes.

Nikki's breathing was shallow and labored. So Branwell laid her down on the floor and started giving her CPR. Vivian came back in, and yelled to Branwell to call 911.

He did, but when he tried to answer the operator,

he couldn't. He tried to speak, but he couldn't. Morris came into the room, and Branwell started to hand him the phone, but Vivian hollered at him to go. She grabbed the phone from Branwell and talked to the emergency operator herself.

"I couldn't utter a sound. I tried to speak, but nothing came out. I knew I was struck dumb as payback for all the times I should have said something and had not. I should have told Tina about all the times I came home from school and found that Vivian had let Nikki's diapers get so wet, the weight made them fall off when you picked her up. I had never said anything about the times I had come home to find Nikki crying while she and Morris stayed in her room, smoking. There were all those times I should have spoken and didn't. I was being punished. And I deserved to be."

So that was how *didn't* speak became *couldn't* speak.

"Bran," I said, "this is the way I look at it. You were struck dumb for a very good reason. Your silence saved Nikki's life."

He smiled. "You're a good friend, Connor. The best friend anyone could ever have, but I'd like to know how you figure that."

"Easy. Logical. As soon as Vivian realized that you

had been struck dumb, she was able to describe to the paramedics and the trauma doctors exactly what she had done—blaming it all on you. She told the medics that *you*—not her—had been rough with Nikki when *you*—not her—went to change Nikki's diaper and *you*—not her—had caused Nikki to hit her head against the tub. *You* had shaken the baby. She knew that she had been taught that shaking can be more dangerous than the fall, and she never would have admitted doing it, but by being able to blame it all on you, she could tell the doctors about it.

"Don't you see? Your silence let her make a confession in your name. She described exactly what happened as if she had witnessed it."

Bran smiled. "Because, of course, she did."

"You didn't hurt Nikki. Vivian did. Something has to be done so that she won't hurt any other babies."

"Probably not even her own . . ."

"If you want that, Bran, you have to file a complaint."

"But I thought you told me that she's in custody. You said that she was picked up after Morris left for work yesterday."

"She was, but if you want her to never be around a baby again, you have to let them know what happened that day of the 911 call."

"No," he said. "I can't. They'll want to know why I *couldn't* speak. And then they'll want to know why I *didn't* speak. And I can't talk about that to anyone else yet."

And that's when I lost it with Bran.

"If you are not willing to tell what happened the day of that 911 call just because you are so ashamed of what happened on Columbus Day, you are stupid and stubborn and you deserve to let Vivian win again."

All he said was, "I can't go home until Nikki does."

And I stormed out of there.

24.

I was in a dilemma. Branwell had not given me permission to tell anyone that he could speak, but it was getting more and more difficult not to. Especially Margaret. When he told me that he would never tell what had happened the day of the 911 call because then everyone would find out what had led up to it, I knew that my silence on the subject would be as bad as his. I had to tell.

So I told Margaret.

She was far more sympathetic to him than I was. "The only way someone as smart and as sensitive as Branwell thinks that he can get the love he so desperately needs is to be good. He feels he has to be good every which way. The way his father wants him to be.

The way The Ancestors want him to be. He could not accept the way he felt about Vivian, and she knew it, and she used it. He needs to learn to accept some intense feelings he has. Like jealousy. And love."

"So what are we going to do?" I asked impatiently.

"We're going to tell Gretchen Silver what Branwell found in the nursery the day he made that 911 call."

Gretchen Silver went to see Branwell the next day. It was his twenty-fifth day at the Behavioral Center.

She insisted that if he wanted to insure that Vivian would never be in a position to hurt another baby, he had to tell her what happened the day of the 911 call. Branwell, who excels at obedience, told.

Gretchen Silver asked the Zamborskas if they wanted to start legal proceedings against Vivian. To spare Branwell from having to testify, Dr. Z decided that he would not pursue the matter in court if the Summerhill Agency, as Vivian Shawcurt's bargaining representative, made certain that she never got a job in child care again. Ever.

Even then, Branwell insisted that he could not go home until Nikki did. Gretchen Silver knew he was as stubborn as he was vulnerable, so she began exploring alternatives.

Finally, after another full day of negotiation, everyone agreed that Branwell would not have to go home. He would go to Margaret's. While there, he would get counseling from Margaret's mother, who said that Branwell had to unload a lot of baggage before moving back to 198 Tower Hill Road anyway. But she would only agree to help Branwell if Dr. Zamborska and Tina got counseling, too.

On December 22 at 1:56 A.M. Greenwich Mean Time, the direct rays of the sun arced over the Tropic of Capricorn, reaching as far south of the equator as they ever go, marking the shortest day of the year and the official start of winter. It was December 21 in Epiphany, and it was evening before Gretchen Silver finally leveled the mountain of paperwork and parted the sea of emotions that allowed Branwell Zamborska to leave the Clarion County Juvenile Behavioral Center.

Before slipping into Margaret's waiting car, Branwell stopped and for the first time in twenty-seven days took in a deep breath of fresh, cold air. Then, with his face as pale as a planet, he looked up at the night sky. "What time is it?" he asked.

"It's eight fifty-six."

"What time is that in London?"

"It's already tomorrow there," Margaret replied.

Branwell smiled. "It's been a long day."

DAY ONE

25.

On the last day of the year, when Branwell had been living on Schuyler Place for ten days, Margaret was making preparations for a small New Year's Eve celebration. She had invited her mother, my mother, The Registrar, and me. I went over there in the middle of the afternoon to help. (I told her that I would set the table since I knew where the silverware was, unless to usher in the new year she had changed her drawers around.)

In the early evening, long before the party was to start, a new minivan pulled into Schuyler Place and parked in front of Margaret's house. Dr. Zamborska got out of the car, walked up the steps and across the front porch, and rang the bell. "Margaret," he said,

"I've come for Branwell."

Margaret called Branwell. He came in from the living room. "Hi, Dad," he said. The four of us filled the narrow hallway between the two front rooms.

Then the front door opened slowly, and Tina walked in. She was carrying Nikki.

Margaret quickly closed the door behind her, and there we all were, standing in the hallway between the two front rooms. No one said anything, and even though I thought I had gotten quite used to silence, this one had a peculiar ache.

Tina pulled back the blanket that had been shielding Nikki's face from the cold, and Nikki looked up and smiled at Branwell, and the silence suddenly seemed musical. And then a sound riffed into that silence. It was Branwell. He was crying. His sobs were soft, cushioned by the long way they had come, the long time they had taken to arrive. He looked at me, then Nikki, then me again, as his tears brightened his face.

And the next thing I knew, I was crying, too. And then we all were. We were all crying except Nikki. She was turning her head this way and that, focusing those black eyes here and there, tracking the sound of sobs and the sight of tears.

At last Tina handed the baby to Branwell. He cradled his little sister in his arms and kissed her until her face was wet with his tears.

Margaret brought out the Kleenex. We all blew our noses and wiped our eyes. Except Branwell. Tina and Dr. Z watched as he tenderly wiped his tears from Nikki's face before he wiped them from his own. And Nikki smiled.

Then Dr. Z said softly to Margaret, "I hope you understand. It's time for us to go home." He looked at Bran holding Nikki and added, "Together."

Tina shook Margaret's hand and said, "It's time."

Dr. Zamborska said, "Get your coat, Bran."

I ran upstairs and got Branwell's jacket. He handed Nikki back to Tina while he put it on. Then, as if it were a given, she handed Nikki back to him.

SIAS: Branwell Zamborska carried his baby sister across the porch, down the stairs, into the minivan and began the first day of the rest of his life.

One *and;* one cliché: four stars.